The Griffin Cryer

Julia Hughes

For Johnny, who also enjoys creating other worlds.

ISBN-13: 978-1482664416
Edited by M Walker,
Talon Publishing.com
Copyright March 2013 Julia Hughes.

PROLOGUE

When the first rider came into view over the horizon, a stab of disappointment pierced the man's chest. It doesn't matter, he thought, there is still time.

He stood at the shore of Troy Lake, conscious of the rays of the setting sun grazing the water's surface before moving away in the direction of the Delphia Mountains, eighty leagues to the east. The rumble of a distant waterfall cascading down the mountain side sounded almost ominous to his ears.

Telluric currents were strong here, making the Wessex ley-line the hardest of all conduits to protect. Several stone monuments—some elaborate, some mere monoliths—stood sentinel between here and the city of the ancient ones, which had been lost to the Uninvited centuries ago. This was the final test for his recruits: to survey the length of the Wessex line, to make certain that the Uninvited were not tampering with the stone monuments which neutralised the ley-line's magnetism: the magnetic forces that kept this world separated from, yet conjoined to, its never-seen twin planet.

Romulus continued to scan the horizon. A second rider came into view, followed by a third. The fourth and fifth riders appeared together some minutes later; and just as the sun slipped behind the mountains, two more recruits rode in. The seven riders dismounted.

The boy was not among them.

Still Romulus kept his vigil. As dusk gave way to complete darkness, the riders' impatient mutterings of discontent became both louder and more frequent, but he paid them no heed.

Inwardly, he sighed. Maybe he had asked too much of the boy: the other recruits were all sons of noblemen, born, as it were, in the saddle. And Balkind had always been a "difficult" ride.

Together, though, Romulus thought that both boy and beast somehow combined to make a team that promised to be something special.

But apparently it wasn't to be. With a heavy heart, the grizzled old warrior signalled to his remaining recruits to mount up. Then, easing himself into his own saddle, he led the way back to camp.

Chapter one.

Taking careful aim, Frankie Shaunessy depressed the trigger, and bullets splurged from the machine gun with a satisfying rattle. Heavyset stern looking men in bullet proof vests and drab uniforms rushed forwards, firing rifles repeatedly. Frankie ducked behind a schoolhouse wall, then lobbed a hand grenade into their midst.

A furious barking drowned out the screams of the injured and dying, Frankie glanced away from the carnage for a split second, but it was enough time for the insurgent: Frankie spun back to face him, as he plunged a combat knife into flesh, between ribs and soft tissue, almost touching the spinal cord. His sneering face filled Frankie's vision; the world melted away and the blood red words "MISSON FAILED ... YOU'RE DEAD!" filled the television's screen.

'Noooo!' Frankie wailed; she'd been so close to the next level.

The frenzied barking continued. 'I'm dead?! Well, so's that bloody dog!' Chucking the X-Box controller onto the coffee table, Frankie bolted out of the house, her red hair streaming behind her.

Bally was dancing with a child-sized woman around the tree in Frankie's next-door-neighbour-but-one's garden. The woman's dressing gown flapped open as she lunged unsuccessfully at the large black dog, who was still barking joyfully. She was also barking: Barking mad.

'Shhhoot!' Frankie glanced back at her house. The curtains in the front bedroom window were closed. She just had to make sure they stayed that way for the next couple of hours: Frankie's step-dad, Tony, worked nights.

Lisa spotted the teenager, still hesitating, and screeched, 'Come and get your bloody dog!'

Of course, next door neighbour Gary and his mates were sitting on the doorstep, smoking a late afternoon cigarette. One of them giggled. 'Come and get your bloody dog,' he repeated shrilly. Frankie's ears burned, but she raised a hand in their direction and managed a grin. Bunch of losers; but they kept the noise down for Tony and never minded if she clambered into their garden after one of Bally's tennis balls.

The moment Frankie entered Lisa's garden, Bally hurtled over, and jumped up to slobber at the girl's face as though he hadn't seen her for days. Frankie grabbed the black Labrador's collar and twisted it, then tapped his nose. 'Quiet, you dopey animal.'

'You want to keep that dog under control,' said Lisa.

Frankie hated her neighbour's smug tone. In fact, she couldn't stand the skinny dried up old cow, with her silly wrist bracelet of faded blue tattoo, and hay for hair – brittle and yellow. She had a strange way of staring into the distance when she spoke, and she was a cat magnet. Every stray in the village ended up in her house.

'Sorry,' Frankie mumbled. She headed for the pavement, dragging Bally along with her. He cast a backwards look at the tree. From the upper branches, a large ginger tom glared down at him, then tipped a leg forward to begin washing itself.

'Allow it Bally, I want to get back to my game.' Frankie rummaged in her tracksuit pockets as she spoke, and *that's* when she remembered she'd carefully replaced the house key in her school bag, ready for tomorrow.

'Shhhoot!' For the second time in as many minutes, Frankie made a conscious effort not to swear. Waking Tony up wasn't an option, and neither was climbing in through a window – not with Gary and his dopey mates watching. As though planned, she spun on her heel and walked in the other direction towards the common, even though the skies were growing dusk.

Behind her, Gary took a last drag of his cigarette, and watched his young neighbour striding away. Frankie's hair provided a vibrant burst of colour as it slapped across the shoulders of her grey tracksuit. In the horizontal rays of the setting sun, she seemed all silver and reddish gold.

Give her a couple of years, and she's going to be a real beauty, Gary thought fondly. Then with a sigh for his own lost youth, he stubbed out his ciggie and went inside to rejoin his mates for their game of bridge.

Frankie's hand rested on Bally's collar as they hiked past gardens filled with late summer flowers: Purple lilacs had already wilted to brown and the last of the roses were fading, while football sized chrysanthemums bloomed with bronze and bright orange petals.

Gardening and gossiping, thought Frankie, that's all there is to do around here. Within ten minutes they were crossing the main road which led to more exciting places than this backward forgotten village. Frankie had already saved over three hundred pounds towards the moped she intended to buy on her sixteenth birthday. She knew her mum would never agree to loan her the money for a motor bike.

Away from the streets and houses, the skies appeared brighter. The footpath skirting the common felt hard and compact after the long dry summer, and Frankie broke into a jog. Bally took this as a signal, and loped off in front of her.

Frankie called him back immediately. Not because she was afraid of ghosts, but she didn't like passing the church lurking at the edge of the common on her own: She didn't like the way tiny solar lights spiked into the ground next to graves shone with a fluorescent glow, she didn't like the uniformed headstones in the war cemetery, and she really didn't like the gargoyle heads leering from the arched window frames. Their ugliness was supposed to scare away evil spirits, but Frankie shuddered each time she passed the medieval relics. Behind the church, the field known locally as "Six Acre Meadow" rose steeply, stretching across to the village centre and the paved road. It had recently been mown, and the golden stubble beckoned invitingly. Vaulting a five bar gate, Frankie decided to cut across the field diagonally, and return home by road. With luck, mum should be home by then, Tony would be having a shower and then they'd all sit down to dinner. Frankie's stomach crooned at the thought of mum's flaky pastry steak pie.

Engrossed in thoughts of home cooking, and wondering if there'd be enough time after dinner to squeeze in another battle on the X-Box, Frankie broached the hill's brow before realising Bally wasn't with her. She pivoted slowly, searching for his darting shadow-like form. Beyond the village a silvery mist rose from the lakes, and began to spread over rooftops, shutting out the streetlamps. The church was invisible, hidden in a slight dip, which was by now filled with mist. If Frankie squinted, she could almost imagine there was a lake; but there was no sign of Bally, frolicking seal like through shards of mist. *Oh dear Lord, I hope he hasn't run home,* she thought, pursing her lips and preparing to call him.

Frankie's first whistle came out as a feeble PHEEP. Licking her lips, she re-pursed them and tried again: Much better! A clear two-tone WHEET-WHOO somewhere between a wolf whistle and a cuckoo's call sang out.

'That bloody dog – nothing but a pain in the backside.' She muttered, and started back down the hill, still whistling. She headed in the direction of the meadow's gate, realising too late that she'd cut in at too steep an angle and almost tumbled over the waist high brick wall enclosing an even older cemetery. These graves dated back to the year dot. Some said even earlier. The inscriptions were long worn away – most of the stone angels had featureless faces. Frankie stopped whistling – it seemed wrong somehow, whistling past the cemetery – and started yelling instead.

'Balkin – Balkin – Baalllkinnnn!' She used the animal's full name to let him know how much trouble he was in now.

On the other side of the wall, tree branches rustled, and then shook as a large shadow lurched forward.

'You bad boy! Get out here quick!' Frankie had a horror of dogs roaming in graveyards, ever since reading one of Ray Bradbury's short stories – the one with the sick boy and the dead teacher.

'Balkin – d'you hear me – get here now!'

She jumped as a wet nose jabbed into her palm, and Bally's head butted against her thigh. Her fingers brushed against velvety fur; sighing with relief, Frankie automatically stroked the silkier hair covering the dog's ear, then froze.

'Bally ...' she squeaked; swallowing hard, she tried again: 'Bally, if you're here – then what on earth is THAT?!'

Without taking her eyes from the shadow, which appeared to be gathering mass, she groped for Bally's collar. The dog whined and struggled, but she held on tight. From somewhere deep within the shadow, large green eyes focused on the teenager – in the centre of the eye, instead of round black pupils, there were only glowing vertical slits of crimson. Frankie's mind urged her to run, but her feet were rooted to the ground. Her heart thundered. Bally whined again, and twisting free from his collar, he raced off towards the main road.

'Bally – no – come back!' Frankie's paralysis melted and she sprinted after him. Commuters used the village as a cut through from one motorway to another. Bally would stand no chance, especially during rush hour. A thunderclap boomed behind, followed by another then another – like a thousand hands applauding in unison. Before Frankie realised it couldn't possibly BE thunder, a blast of hot fetid air knocked her to the ground. Seconds later, a sail-sized leathery wing swept past, trailed by a raggedy tail which ended in a spike. A hoarse bellow filled the darkening sky.

A DRAGON – IT'S A DRAGON – Frankie's mind jabbered. Clutching her hands over her ears, she curled up in a ball and waited for the world to end.

From a distance, Frankie heard someone calling Balkin's name over the sound of her own heartbeat, and forced herself to sit up.

'Please God, let someone catch him before he gets to the main road.' She moaned out-loud: oR GETS EATEN BY THE DRAGON, her mind added.

'Balkind – come back!' A man wearing fancy dress topped with a white blond wig stepped over the churchyard wall. With his head tilted heavenward, he didn't notice the cowering teenager until he stumbled over Frankie's feet. He glared down. His eyes were the darkest shade of blue – almost navy – and deep set under his dark blond eyebrows. Both colours were startling against his dark skin.

'Did you summons my griffin?'

Frankie gaped at the vision, scootching a little further away, still on her hands and bottom.

'What?'

With a sigh of impatience, he lunged. Frankie threw up her arms in defence, but it seemed the stranger only wanted to stand her upright. Keeping his hands on her shoulders, he shook her to and fro, as though trying to shake an answer from her.

'You summoned my griffin. You whistled three times, then called three times – yes?'

'What?'

'My griffin!' He gestured helplessly at the fast-disappearing dragon, now a speck in the distance.

Frankie stared at him open mouthed. The local drama group met on Tuesday, two whole days ago, and she hadn't seen anyone else wearing fancy dress. The stranger wore a thigh-length leather waistcoat affair over a vest of some kind. His trousers seemed to be made of a pale woollen material, though it was hard to tell: from ankle to knee he'd wrapped a leather strapping around them. There were similar, though wider, leather straps around his forearms. His hair swept behind his neck, and disappeared into a scarlet cloak that hung from his shoulders.

Frankie opened and shut her mouth, unable to think of a single thing to say. Finally she managed: 'Get lost, you madman!' Scowling, he took a step towards her, reaching behind his shoulders with one hand, murder in his face. Wishing she'd bitten off her tongue before insulting him, then realising she still clutched at Balkin's collar; Frankie chucked it with all her might and scored a lucky hit right between his eyes.

He staggered backwards, throwing his hands up to his face, and yelling what sounded like a curse – but Frankie didn't stop to ask for a translation. Tucking her head into her chin, she sprinted to the gate and threw herself over. She pushed past brambles and stinging nettles, and sprinted straight across the common, running for her life. The grassy path wasn't much more than a rut, worn down by dog walkers, but it was a short cut. She didn't dare look back, but she could hear footsteps, growing louder as the stranger gained on her.

Then she heard something that chilled her blood. A swoosh of displaced air whistled behind her calves, causing filament hairs to stand on end. Without breaking pace, Frankie ducked her head even lower to peer under her arm, and her heart skipped a beat. The madman was only feet away, and he was WAVING A SWORD AT HER.

From somewhere Frankie found extra speed. She cleared the ditch and pushed through the hedge to emerge at the roadside. She teetered there for a moment, pin wheeling her arms for balance. A cry of surprise from behind indicated her pursuer had discovered the ditch.

Luck was with Frankie. Four cars whizzed by in quick succession; the next vehicle, a skip lorry, was still thirty yards distant. She darted across the road in front of it, to where a bus had just halted to pick up passengers. Having reached civilization, she felt safer. She stopped to catch her breath, and looked back.

On the other side of the road, the common appeared as a pitch black hole. Through a gap in the traffic, Frankie saw the hedge part, and a mass of pale blond hair emerged. A car's headlight glinted off metal – he must still be waving that sword around. A stream of traffic flashed by; in each oncoming vehicle's headlights Frankie caught only flickering images of the stranger, and she laughed. She laughed at the look of surprise on his face, then the look of horror, and finally fear. Another gap in the traffic revealed he no longer had the sword in his hand. Frankie couldn't see his face without the headlights, but knew he was looking at her. She couldn't see his expression either, but his body language spoke of total disgust. He turned his back, and pushed back through the hedge, disappearing into the darkness.

With a sob of relief, Frankie turned for home, hoping against hope Bally would be waiting for her there. Instead, when she arrived around ten minutes later, she found that World War Three had broken out.

Tony, still in his boxers and vest, clutched Frankie's mum round the waist, trying to drag her away from Lisa's garden gate. Screeching, her mum slapped at his hands in a bid to escape his grasp. Her feet scrabbled to find purchase. She yelled at Tony, and yelled at the mad old cat woman. Lisa stood calmly in her garden, arms crossed and smirking. Gary had her mum's other side, and though other neighbours were streaming from their houses or gaping from their windows, Frankie's mum kept screaming – mainly at Tony to set her down.

'Let go of me! I'm going to kill her, the evil old cow!'

All three front doors were wide open, and there was no sign of Bally. Frankie raced towards her mum and Tony, but one of Gary's mates rugby-tackled Frankie and started to carry her into her house. Tony backed down the path, half-dragging, half-carrying mum. Gary's friend held Frankie in a sort of half-nelson, but she wouldn't be budged from the doorway.

'Mum, what's going on?' Frankie shouted. 'What's she done?'

Gary took action now. He strode into Lisa's garden, picked her up, and threw her through her own front door, then slammed it shut, yelling, 'Stay in there you muck-stirring old bitch.'

Giving a nod to Tony, Gary dusted his palms together with satisfaction and raised his eyebrows at his mate, jerking his head to say "come on leave it now," and went indoors. And that was that. Mum collapsed against Tony, who helped her into the house.

'Put the kettle on,' Tony said, and Frankie rushed to obey, wondering what on earth had just happened. On the kitchen table were three plates, bright green broccoli had just been strained, and peering into a saucepan she saw a heap of greying potatoes, the water that had been covering them completely boiled away. At least someone had turned off the oven, so hopefully the pies hadn't burned to a cinder.

With the kettle filled and switched on, Frankie rushed back into the front room. Her mum sat on the sofa's edge, with her head buried in her hands, sobbing. Kneeling in front of her, Frankie tried to pull her hands away from her eyes.

'Mum, please, you're scaring me – what's happened?'

Tony spoke in a rough growl. 'It's Bally.'

Frankie closed her eyes in anticipation of his next words: "He's dead." But instead she heard, 'That old witch found him running around in the road, and called the K-9 Dogs' Home.'

Frankie gaped at him. 'What?'

'They won't give him back – they won't give him back until tomorrow.' Mum said between sobs. Frankie breathed again.

Tony's voice rumbled on: 'Lisa knew very well we wouldn't get him back after four. Admin's gone home, and the dog catcher won't release any dog without official permission.'

'She's wicked, Tony – wicked – poor old Bally – he'll be wondering what's happening.' Between sobs she hiccupped 'He'll think he's been abandoned.'

'Come on love, chin up. He'll be home tomorrow. Frankie – is that kettle boiling yet? Make your mum a cuppa, and I'll nip over the chippies and get some chips.'

Dinner was a sullen silent meal. Tony left his half eaten, in a rush not to be late for work. Mum scrapped the left-overs into Bally's bowl, and started crying again. Frankie tried to comfort her with a hug, only to be rebuffed and snapped at for not putting Bally's collar and lead on. Then mum shouted at Frankie again for treading dog's mess into the house. Frankie didn't shout back, instead, she mentally counted to ten. Then she cleaned the dog's muck from the welcome mat, gritting her teeth and trying not to breath in the odour. By the time she'd finished, mum had unzipped her brief case and the sofa and coffee table was covered with paperwork, while mum scowled over columns of sums. There didn't seem any point in asking for the telly to be switched on, even if she promised to keep the sound down. Trudging upstairs, Frankie took a long hot shower, and climbed into bed.

Her head buzzed, and her chest hurt. It was easier to let the tears fall down her face. They flowed down her cheeks, and dripped from her chin into the little hollow at her throat, stinging her skin as they dried. *This is all my fault. Stupid stupid stupid: Seeing dragons and swordsmen in the dark.* Closing her eyes, Frankie wondered if somehow she'd imagined the whole thing. It really wouldn't surprise her. After all, she'd even managed to get the physics back to front – first the wind knocking her over THEN the dragon sweeping past. "Griffin – not dragon: griffin – and it has to flap its wings a few times to build up momentum for flight." A small voice in her mind corrected. Frankie's eyes flew open – that explained the blast of displaced air that knocked her down. She closed her eyes again, only to see Bally, cowering in some grotty kennel, raising his eyes dolefully at every sound, hoping to see *his* humans. Sobbing even harder, Frankie pulled the duvet over her head and fell into an exhausted sleep.

Chapter two.

"Griffin tears are believed to have the power to heal even the most grievous of wounds."

Frankie's math teacher, Martin "Sarky" Sharky, paced the classroom as he spoke, waving her rough notes around like the Olympic torch. Chelsi Morgan gave Frankie a look of phony sympathy, and the rest of the class giggled.

Mr Sharky then moved to the centre of the room, rocked back on his heel, and pivoted slowly through 360 degrees so everyone could see his smile of derision. Then he faced Frankie again.

'"Griffin tears," Francesca Shaunessy? Can you explain what "*Griffin tears*" have to do with algebra?'

Frankie stood in front of her desk, knowing her classmates' eyes were on her, hoping she'd start crying, or at least blush.

'I finished my worksheet,' she mumbled. 'I'm writing an essay on mythical beasts for English homework.'

His hamster-like cheeks bulged even more. 'Homework? You're doing *English* homework in *my* class?' He screwed the piece of paper up into a ball and aimed it at the wastepaper bin. It hit the rim and bounced back, setting off another round of giggles.

Mr Sharky's face flushed with embarrassment, and he took it out on Frankie.

'Stay behind when class is dismissed. You can spend the entire lunch-hour writing lines.'

In her blazer pocket, Frankie's hand curled around the note giving her permission to go home at midday. Mum had scribbled it out over breakfast; by now she should have rung the dogs' home to explain her daughter would be collecting Bally.

'Sir I can't, I've got a note – I'm going home at lunch time.'

Wordlessly he held out his hand. Mr Sharky's lips moved as he read, reminding Frankie even more of a hamster nibbling on a sunflower seed. His sarcasm soared. 'Of course, visiting the local dogs' home is *so* much more important than your education. Okay Miss Shaunessy. You can sit down now. Tell your parents you'll be late home on Monday. You've got two hours detention after school.'

As though Frankie hadn't suffered enough humiliation, Chelsi Morgan defended her:

'Sir, Frankie has to pick up her brother's dog.'

Now *all* the eyes that were on Frankie were pitying. *Don't look at me like that, don't feel sorry for me. Mikey's still alive, my brother isn't dead yet. Where there's life there's hope*, Frankie told herself fiercely.

Poppy, Chelsi's best mate, whispered to her – in a fake whisper designed to be overheard – 'Maybe that's why she was reading about griffin tears you know...'

'Don't be ridiculous Poppy," Mr Sharky admonished, without bothering to turn his head, so missing the evil glare Poppy gave him, then Frankie.

Slapping her mum's scribbled note onto Frankie's desk, Mr Sharky's cheeks twitched as he gave her a final smirk, and then stalked back to the board. He began writing out equations, pressing the marker so hard against the white board that it squeaked. Beside Frankie, Annette whispered 'sorry.'

Frankie ignored her. Obviously she'd told her best friend that she wouldn't be in afternoon lessons, and why. Frankie hadn't asked Annette to keep it a secret; she'd just assumed Annette wouldn't mouth off to Chelsi and her set.

The bell rang, followed by the clatter of thirty chairs being scraped away from desks.

'Sit down.'

'But sir, we'll be late for lunch.'

'Thank Miss Shaunessy.' Mr Sharky tapped at the board. 'This is your homework for the weekend. Copy out these questions and hand your answers into the staff room first thing Monday morning.' The class groaned.

'Thank Miss Shaunessy.' The sarcastic teacher repeated and, smiling like the joker out of *Batman*, he strolled between desks, twirling the pen in the air and catching it as he went. The metal door squeaked a complaint as he left the room, and Frankie to her classmates' scorn.

'Way to go Frankfurter.' Even the class nerds muttered under their breath as they scurried out the room. Peter Roberts stopped at Frankie's desk.

'You're doing my bloody homework,' he said, 'and you better make sure you get it right.'

He shoved Frankie's head down against the desk as he left, uttering a swear-word that made her cheeks sting.

'Pete! Don't be so crude.' Chelsi hurried after him, flashing Frankie another look of fake sympathy as she went.

Frankie hated them both; Chelsi more than her foul mouthed boyfriend. If she lived in America, she would be chief cheerleader. Sadly for Chelsi, she lived in nowhere-ville, but that didn't stop her wearing short skirts and tight jumpers and jumping up and down manically so her long blonde hair swished and swirled like some silly shampoo advert every time Pete and his stupid football team scored a goal.

Annette remained seated in silent solidarity. Frankie swung her hair forward, creating a curtain between them.

'Frankie, I'm so sorry – you didn't say *not* to say anything.'

'That's because I didn't think you'd rush over to that lot and start mouthing off about me and my family.'

'I'm sorry Frankie, they just wanted to know where you were at breaktime, and one thing led to another and next thing I was telling them about Bally going missing – I'm sorry Frankie.'

Refusing to look at her, Frankie swept out the classroom, keeping her head high and blinking back tears.

It doesn't matter, she told herself, it doesn't matter. Only ninety-eight days to go and I'll be sixteen and no-one will ever be able to tell me when to stand up and sit down so they can bawl me out in front of a whole classroom again.

But right now, she was free from school for hours and hours and hours, and even better, wouldn't have maths again until Wednesday.

Frankie squeezed past a gaggle of sixth formers mooching around the lockers chatting about their plans for the weekend. Their tie-less shirts hung outside their trousers, just to show they were rebels – rebels who chose to return to this sink-hole as sixth formers rather than try for a half decent college – and then she almost tripped over a little Year 8, bent double, tying his shoelace.

'Sorry sorry, can't stop!' Frankie continued with her dash to the bus stop. Behind her the rebel sixth formers cat-called and a shrill voice screamed 'I'm telling my brother you knocked me flying – you clumsy cow!'

But Frankie didn't care – the bus was only thirty yards away from the stop outside the school gates, and she ran like the hounds of hell were behind her to catch it.

Once on board, Frankie began to relax. In twenty minutes, she'd be reunited with Bally. He'll be so pleased to see me, she thought – and then realised suddenly she hadn't brought his lead, or even any money. *Never mind, mum will have sorted that all out over the phone,* she comforted herself, gazing out the window as green fields bordered by darker green trees flashed by. This long straight stretch of country road met with the M40 motorway a few miles up ahead, and though the speed limit had recently been reduced to fifty miles an hour, even bus drivers still behaved as though they were on a race track. Although in Frankie's view, too fast was never fast enough, and especially not today. *Not long now, and I'll be walking Bally home through those fields, back across country,* and her barely there reflection grinned back at her.

As though conjured up by her mind, Frankie caught a fleeting glimpse of a dog that could easily have been Bally's double, loping along with its master. Before she could look closer, they'd vanished into the woods.

There wasn't an official halt outside the dogs' home, but the driver pulled up at the mouth of the drive. Several posters advertised happy looking dogs of all shapes and sizes, from the clowns of the dog world, Jack Russells, to an aristocratic Afghan Hound. Hoisting her rucksack higher onto her shoulder, wishing she'd thought to at least bring a couple of biscuits for Bally, Frankie began walking down the long drive. Sometimes, while walking in the woods, she could hear a crescendo of barking, but not today. Frankie stepped aside as a blue estate car drove past, a man at the wheel, a woman next to him. Sandwiched between two kids in the back seat, a collie type sat to attention. Its ears pricked and its tongue lolled with delight, while the kids enthusiastically patted his coat. Feeling a sudden spasm of loneliness, Frankie walked on.

The purpose built kennel blocks were located behind a converted farmhouse, which served as administration offices, while upstairs had been converted into a grounds' keeper's flat. Despite Frankie's visions of Bally shivering in squalor, this place was a canine five star hotel: Each kennel was supposed to be the size of a single bedroom, and have under floor heating. Or so Frankie had been told: although the home held open days and dog shows, and was just a couple of miles outside the village, this was Frankie's first visit.

There were only four vehicles parked in one corner of the staff car-park, two of them dog wardens' vans, but the visitors' car park was full. With a feeling of queasiness, Frankie realised they weren't all here to choose a dog. There were tea-rooms at this place, and people visited just to walk around the kennels, to ooh and ahh over the "dear little doggies": the sort of people who also went to zoos to point at the monkeys and shudder at the reptile house. Michael used to laugh when his sister mouthed off about animals in captivity, pointing out that it kept the money rolling in and the animals relatively safe. Then he'd pretend to be serious and ask if Frankie had plans to campaign for goldfish to be liberated from their bowls.

'Can I be of any help?'
Frankie shook out of the daydream – the question was delivered in the pained tones of someone who'd been forced to repeat themselves – and smiled at the elderly woman perched behind a wide wooden counter. Frankie decided there must be a hairdressers somewhere especially for little old ladies; why else would they all have the same blue tinged cauliflower hair style? Collecting herself, she said:
'Hi, I'm Francesca Shaunessy, my mum called earlier – I'm here to pick up my dog.' Frankie grinned as she said his name: 'Bally, he's a black Labrador.'
Raising her eyebrows, the clerk looked Frankie up and down, then wrinkled her brow.
' – do you mean Ballykinny Lad? He's gone. Your brother collected him barely half an hour ago.'

'What?' Frankie clutched at the counter. For one heart stopping moment she believed the old woman. Michael had disconnected his drips and monitors, and clambering over the sides of his cot-like bed come to claim his dog.

As if talking to a simpleton the woman repeated 'Your brother – Frankie Shaunessy,' the furrows on her brow deepened.

'You don't look much like brother and sister. Frankie and Francesca eh?' Abruptly she jumped from her stool, even smaller standing than she was sitting, and hurried around to Frankie's side of the counter. Cupping an elbow, she guided Frankie over to a chair.

'Are you feeling alright? You've turned white as a sheet.' Resisting the pressure to sit down, Frankie shook the woman's hand off.

'No I'm not all right. I'm Frankie – Francesca Shaunessy – you've given my dog away to some randomer who wandered in off the street.'

The clerk's lips tightened as she realised what she'd done.

'I'm so sorry – he had a collar with the dog's identity disc on it – asked if we'd had a large black dog handed in. We only had one black dog by the name of Ballykinny Lad – and we'd already been told by Mrs Shaunessy that her daughter Frankie would be along mid-day to collect him.'

Daughter! Her daughter!'

'Don't shout at me, young lady. I assumed someone had got the message wrong. He knew the dog's name, *and* he had the collar and ID disc. He even said if a red haired girl shows up, asking for the dog, tell her I'll meet her at the usual place.'

'What?'

'The word is "pardon," not "what." He said ...'

Frankie didn't wait to hear the rest. This was no random stranger. This was *her* stranger.

Chapter three.

A man sat outlined against the brow of Six Acre Meadow, a large black dog by his side. Frankie stumbled towards them, clutching at the stitch in her side. By the time she reached the top of the hill and stood over him, all the furious insults she'd rehearsed on the nightmare jog here were useless. Instead she glared down at him, struggling to catch her breath. Bally's tail thumped, but he made no attempt to cease worrying at the mammoth bone he held down with one paw.

Finally Frankie managed: 'That's my dog.'

Calmly unscrewing the lid from a bottle of water, the stranger took a couple of swigs, then offered it to Frankie. After a moment's hesitation, she swiped the bottle from him, tipped her head back, and chugged down.

'Where's my griffin?' the man asked.

Frankie clutched the now empty bottle, longing to chuck it at his head and snatch up Bally and run. But somehow she doubted his temper had improved any since last night.

'Please – I don't know your name – but please – let me have my dog back. Please – it'll break my mum's heart.'

'Get me back my griffin and you can have your dog.'

'I'll call the police.'

He shrugged, looking completely unconcerned. 'Call for my griffin, and you can have your dog back.'

Frankie gave a sigh of surrender, and tossed the empty bottle neatly into his opened rucksack.

'If I call your ...griffin – and it doesn't come, will that satisfy you?'

He nodded. 'If you call with all your heart, and Balkind doesn't answer, you may have your dog back.'

Call with all your heart. Frankie knew without asking what this meant. Inflating her lungs, and placing her hands either side of her mouth, she summoned up a cry from the heart.

'Balkind!'

The sound flooded the meadow. Frankie sucked in air and called again. 'Baalll-kind.' She could feel two pairs of eyes on her, watching intently, Bally's ears were pricked. Before calling for the third time, Frankie took a couple of steps away from her audience, and focussed on projecting her cry across the village, across the lakes, across the country if needs be.

'Baaaalllll-kiiiiinnnnnd!'

Frankie glanced behind her. The blond head nodded approval.

'That'll do.'

Of course it would: Any griffin within a hundred miles would have heard that.

'What now?'

The man jerked his head towards Bally. 'Take him.' He sat with his hands resting loosely on bent knees. Then with a casual glance at the horizon, he rummaged in the bag at his side, drew out another meaty bone, and began to gnaw on it.

Frankie stared. He glanced up, and tipped the bone towards her. 'Sorry – would you like some?'

'No thank you.' Frankie responded with equal politeness. Her eyes flickered towards the churchyard and he laughed, patting the ground beside him.

'Sit down. You really need to control your imagination.'

Right. A sword wielding weirdo who owns a griffin and likes his meat raw telling me to curb my imagination. But Frankie sat down, careful not to sit too close.

The meadow's stubble prickled at her thighs, bare beneath her grey school skirt. Frankie shrugged off her maroon blazer, spread it out beneath her, and stretched her legs out flat.

Her stomach rumbled, embarrassingly loudly. She could murder a ham sandwich or even a packet of crisps right now. Beside her, the bone-crunching continued in unison. At least only Bally was drooling. Frankie couldn't stand this any longer.

'How can you eat that?' She blurted.

He shrugged 'I'd prefer it cooked. But I don't have my fire maker with me.'

'Oh.' She glanced sideways. He'd cracked the bone open, and inside was a pinkish grey filling. He scooped it out and into his mouth with his fingers. Frankie noticed he swallowed without chewing.

'You mean your griffin can breath fire?' She asked.

'No. Of course he doesn't breathe fire. I mean I've left my fire makings behind.' He waved the bone splinter towards the church. Then he swiped his hand across his mouth and tossed the bone to Bally, and grimaced.

'Got to keep my strength up.'

Frankie didn't know if he was joking or not. Twigs festooned his hair, his face still had smears of mud and traces of blood, but at least he'd lost the dungeons and dragons outfit. Wearing baggy khaki shorts and an even baggier tee-shirt, he looked like a grunger, or a new-ager, but if he cleaned his face, he probably wouldn't attract a second glance in a crowd.

Frankie glanced across rooftops to the horizon. On this typical early September day, the sky seemed painted blue. A red kite floated lazily over the common; if it drifted toward the crows' nursery, over to their left, the crows would rise up in unison and drive the intruder away. Frankie turned back to the man.

'What's going on?' She asked him. 'Last night you were chasing me with a sword, today you're totally chilled.'

He frowned. 'It was a little cold last night, and I felt a chill this morning – but now…'

'I mean – you seem relaxed – not disturbed.'

'Last night I was returning home when Balkind vanished into a mist. I went after him and found you gibbering like an idiot and Balkind flying off frightened out of his wits.'

He glanced at Frankie's short skirt and pale freckled legs. 'Besides, I thought you were a knave. You certainly cursed like a knave. I didn't realise you were just a little girl.'

'I am NOT a little girl! I'm nearly sixteen years old.'

'That many years!' he mocked, clearly enjoying Frankie's anger.

'How old are you?'

'Old enough to respect my elders,' he said. This guy really did have a talent for pushing buttons, Frankie thought.

'So just because someone's old I should respect them?'

'Since older people have laboured longer and usually have more gold – then yes – I would say yes.'

'So just because they're older, and richer, I should respect them?'

'Because they've laboured longer, to provide for their children and their children's children. Yes. I believe so.'

He stood suddenly, shading his eyes with one hand. 'Your griffin's answered your cry.' Stooping, he placed a hand under Frankie's elbow and helped her to her feet. His smile was wide and his eyes full of warmth, and for the first time, Frankie found herself liking him.

But there was no time to think about that. Frankie followed the man's gaze and saw that Balkind *had* answered her cry. His wings barely flapped as he rode the thermals. As he neared them he dropped his equine shaped head, and a strange hoarse bellow filled the air again. He circled, a mere forty feet above Frankie and his owner now. His wings flapped, like a sailboat tacking against the wind. Pointing his snout earthwards, and with forearms outstretched to brace against the ground, he touched down twenty feet away. Frankie clutched at the stranger for dear life.

'There, not so frightening this time was it?' the man laughed, his happiness infectious, and Frankie laughed too, as Balkind folded the last of his wing span concertina like against his flanks. With his wings tucked neatly behind his forelegs, his long body undulated and his neck curled so his chin almost touched his chest, and he snorted with pleasure and underfoot the earth rumbled as he gambolled over with an odd shuffling motion to greet his owner and Frankie. 'May I…touch him?' she asked. The man nodded.

The texture of Balkind's skin was a mixture of satin and silkiness. A dense pewter coloured fur covered his neck and head, which shimmered in the sunlight as his eyes darted from Frankie, to his master, then to Bally, breathing in the unique scent of each of them. Two barley sugar horns protruded from his head, and his gossamer wings were almost invisible against his flanks. His tail thrashed from side to side. That he was pleased to be amongst friends again was obvious. Frankie turned to the stranger.

'Do griffin tears have healing powers?'

She blurted the words out without thinking:

The man looked at her, his strange blue eyes filled with scorn.

'You ask the silliest questions. I expect your tutors fight or draw straws over who is to learn you lessons.'

'The only silly question is the one you don't ask.' Frankie said, 'besides, it's *teach* lessons, not learn.'

'Maybe so, but before speaking, you should ask yourself the question again, only slower.' He turned away and rummaged in his bag again, adding 'I'm not surprised you don't learn.' Both dog and griffin stilled with anticipation as he dragged out another bone. Frankie sincerely hoped he hadn't robbed the graveyard. With exaggerated calmness she repeated slowly:

'Do griffin tears have healing powers?'

'Yes of course. Just one tear could bring this bone back to life.' Then he tossed the bone to Balkind, who caught it in his jaws.

'Don't mess with me!' Frankie warned – wishing she *were* a knave – She'd knock that silly smile off his face double quick! The man ignored her. Feeling about eight years old again, Frankie turned her attention to his griffin. In a similar fashion to Bally, Balkind held the bone steady with one fearsome looking talon while he crunched it down in two bites. His floppy upper lip curled backwards, displaying long canine teeth also similar to Bally's.

Bally watched the bone disappear, he looked confused, as though to say *where'd it go?* Then he nudged at the rucksack, giving hopeful glances up to his new human friend, who was obviously thinking the same as Frankie. 'Balkind and Balkin.' He mused, as Balkind ducked his head and placed his nostrils against Bally's broad head, sniffing as though he could eat the smell of dog.

'Balkin's short for Ballykinny Lad. We call him Bally for shorter,' Frankie explained. For years Michael had wanted a dog, comparing breeds and taking on extra newspaper rounds, and never missing a chance to bore anyone who cared to listen about what he was going to call his dog, and the hikes they'd have over mountains and wild places.

Canine Balkin snapped at griffin Balkind's nose, and with a final snort of disgust, Balkind whipped his head away, swivelling on that long muscular neck, and, without warning, thrust it into Frankie's chest.

Automatically her arms went up, and she found herself stroking, burying her finger tips in velveteen fur. She found his soft spot, right between the barley sugar horns, and knuckled the spot there. His eyes closed with bliss and a deep rumble shook his body, deepening until it shimmered against Frankie's bones.

'He's purring.' Her arms were beginning to ache.

Shaking his head but still smiling, the stranger reached up and scratched the side of the griffin's neck where it emerged from his shoulder, and with a sort of collapsing at his knees, Balkind fell to the ground. Frankie half expected him to roll over onto his back.

Balkind's owner flopped to the ground to sit just above the griffin, out of danger if Balkind did decide to roll. Frankie sat a little closer, and it seemed natural when Balkind stretched out his neck and placed his head in her lap. When Frankie expressed surprise at its lightness, the griffin's owner said: 'Their bones are hollow. We feed them a special diet.'

Frankie wondered just how many griffins he owned, and if he'd used the "Royal We" or if there were more like him back home, but more importantly, she wanted to know more about this "special diet".

'Really?' She asked.

'Hmm.' He didn't elaborate.

Frankie continued stroking, and the rumbling purr started up again. With a grunt, Bally laid his head on the stranger's knee, and they could have been any ordinary couple out for a walk with their dog. And griffin.

'So what do they eat?'

'Mainly sixteen year old maidens.' He teased. Frankie reached across and punched him.

'Joker.'

'Joker? Oh – jester.' He seemed amused and content to just sit there, shooting the breeze.

'What are you waiting for, don't you want to go home' – it sounded strange to say it, but she said it anyway – 'back to your own world?'

He grimaced. 'I've tried. I've been back to... ' he waved towards the woods and the boundary of the church wall. 'Last night I heard Balkind preparing to fly, and a scream – and I rushed forward blindly – straight into a pillar of stone carved like a figure with wings. So I went back to that point.' He shrugged, 'the portal, the opening between worlds isn't there.'

Frankie stared at him. 'So you can't get back?'

'I'm waiting for dusk. The curtain between worlds is thinner at sunrise and sunset.' He sounded nonchalant. A thought struck Frankie, and forgetting the stranger's recent advice she blurted:

'Didn't you try this morning?' He didn't answer, but his silence spoke for him.

'I don't understand – how can you sit there so calmly?'

'What would you have me do? Throw rocks at the sun to move it through the sky faster?'

Frankie realised she'd angered him somehow, perhaps he wasn't as confident as he appeared to be. He made a visible effort to control his temper, and went on more evenly. 'I can't allow myself to panic. There are stories; others from our world have visited yours and returned, and we have had visitors from your world who have "magically" disappeared.'

Reaching over, he chucked Frankie under the chin, as if to say "friends again?", dropping his hand to stroke Balkind, now half asleep.

And in that moment, for the first time Frankie believed in him. Until then, she'd been sub-consciously waiting for the punch line – half expecting the eager beaver director of this crazy reality show to jump out and confess to an elaborate prank. She felt incredibly sorry for him, and incredibly amazed at his bravery.

'Why did Balkind come when I called?'

'You have the gift. You're a "Griffin Cryer."'

'A "Griffin Cryer?" Then why has he never come before when I called for Bally?'

He shrugged. 'I don't know. Why don't you ask him? Maybe he never heard you calling before.'

Frankie considered this, and it seemed to make sense. She sat there, stroking a griffin's head, making small talk with some other-worlder, and it seemed to make sense. She felt more at ease with this stranger than with Annette, for some reason. Apart from the hollowness in her stomach, she could sit here all day. The afternoon sun shone down, and Frankie slowly rehearsed in her mind the questions she wanted to ask her new friend.

Bally stiffened to attention suddenly, and without troubling to get up, gave his "welcome" bark.

'Watcha Frankie! That's some ugly horse you've got there!' Postie John hiked by on sturdy shorts-clad legs, his morning round over, on his way back to the postmistress.

Frankie managed to stutter a reply, but she was talking to his back, and he didn't respond.

'Horse? Is he blind and deaf?'

Frankie giggled nervously. As usual, John wore his earphones, and was probably listening to his beloved heavy metal music. Nice bloke, tragic taste in music. 'I suppose if you weren't expecting to see a griffin, your first thought would be horse.'

'Nonsense. The man's an idiot. Balkind has two horns, not one.'

'Wha – I mean, pardon?'

'Say "what did you say?" if you didn't hear or understand me. "Pardon" is for if you accidentally step on my foot.'

'What?'

'Pardon is for when you step on my foot.' He repeated patiently, and Frankie couldn't resist. The effect wasn't so good from a sitting position, but she managed to kick at his bare instep. 'Pardon.' Before she could shove Balkind from her lap and take off down the meadow, he pounced. Pinning her shoulders to the ground with one knee, he put her head in a vice, and knuckled the top of Frankie's skull until she begged for mercy between shouts and giggles and Bally licking her face.

Finally the torture stopped. Still catching her breath between snorts of laughter, Frankie stood up, straightening her skirt and dusting off grass stains. Balkind watched with disdain, Bally did his "thank goodness we're on the move again" dance and the stranger reclined back on his elbows, as though he hadn't reduced her to an undignified heap of giggling schoolgirl.

'I'll get you for that.' Frankie warned.

He closed his eyes to show his contempt for this threat. So she trampled on his stomach, only a gentle stamp, enough to knock the wind from him and to give herself a chance to escape. Even winded, he caught her foot and before the squeal left her lips, Frankie's heels whizzed over her head and she landed flat on her back.

'No – I'm sorry – I'm sorry – I didn't mean it!' She raised her hands defensively, screwing up her eyelids and cringing against the torment coming her way. Bally's barking grew more frantic. When Frankie opened her eyes again, she saw his face hovering over hers, and his eyes had darkened to midnight blue. Rolling away, he sat up abruptly. 'You'd better go on home now, little girl.'

Frankie frowned, they were only having a game weren't they? Did he actually think she wanted him to kiss her or something? Her cheeks felt hot, how arrogant – *little girl* indeed! He couldn't be more than seventeen or eighteen himself!

'Allow you! I'm going!' And she stormed off down the slope, Bally by her side, sensing that playtime was over. Behind her, Balkind bellowed his distress. A couple of figures pottering around in the churchyard paused in their grave tending and froze, fear on their faces as they spotted the outline of a griffin.

'Realistic isn't it?' Frankie said, relieved when the two middle aged women, obviously sisters in their look alike pink trousers and matching tops, exchanged rueful glances with each other then smiled and agreed with her. Spinning on her heel, Frankie marched back up the hill to the rudest man in this world or any other and the sweetest griffin she'd ever met.

Bally danced with delight, then charged away to his new friends. Alerted to her return, the arrogant stranger sat up, putting an arm around Bally, the traitor dog.

'Back again, did you forget something? Your manners, perchance?'

Frankie scowled, 'You can't stay here. You're freaking out the natives. Take Balkind and wait for dusk in those woods over there – you don't want to be seen.'

'Why not? Though I suppose if all your villagers ask the same silly questions as you, it could become tiresome.' He yawned and stretched to show how tiresome he found her.

'Look – go and hide in the woods, right? Do you want Balkind to be taken away from you and put in a circus or something?'

He snorted with amusement. 'Anyone who wants Balkind can have eight inches of my sword first.' But he got to his feet, scratching Balkind's shoulder again, which seemed to be a signal.

The woods ran behind the churchyard, skirting the meadow. These were the same woods that Frankie had seen from the bus window. It was possible to walk almost to the neighbouring town through them. Frankie recalled reading that at one time, a squirrel could travel the length of the kingdom without setting foot on the ground. Two years ago, on a package holiday to Rome, she'd peered from the airplane's window, astounded by the expanse of greenery that still covered this little island.

'Let's not part bad friends, I beg your pardon for any offence given. Walk with me.' He said, and since it wasn't out of her way, Frankie nodded agreement. Her hand rested on Balkind's flank, and she wondered suddenly how it would be to soar through the air with the wind whipping through her hair; it must be a feeling of total freedom. Her heart hammered faster at the thought.

'Would you like a ride on your griffin?'

She looked up, startled. 'Can you read minds?'

'No, but your thoughts are so transparent, they're written in your face. Would you like to ride Balkind?'

Frankie shook her head, no, when she wanted to yell yes.

'It's more important for you to get back to your world. So far we – I mean – you've been lucky – but you can't take any risks.'

They'd reached the edge of the woods now, a rabbit path opened up, and Frankie led the way. The path skirted a swampy mess, one of a few lurking in these woods, before joining a wider path.

Frankie pointed to the other side of the swamp, towards a grove of chestnut trees. 'If you wait there until dusk, no-one will see you.'

Already the brambles had sprung back; there was no sign that a griffin had passed this way.

'So this is goodbye then Francesca.'

It was the first time he'd spoken her name. She felt tearful suddenly. She nodded, 'This is goodbye.' She realised she didn't know his name.

'If I tell you my name, do you promise never to call me?' He teased, Frankie looked up at him with a startled expression. Bemused even further when he stroked her face with his fingers, circling it from temple to chin. 'Your thoughts show too clearly. Now you are a big girl, you must learn to hide them.' Frankie slapped his hand away, half angry, half laughing.

'I promise.'

'My name is Balkind's Rider.' And laughing out loud, he strode off, calling behind him 'Come Balkind.' With a last look at Frankie, Balkind followed obediently. No doubt he didn't want to be lost and alone again.

Frankie stomped off in the other direction, heading for home, too angry to feel any sense of loss at parting from her griffin. *Tomorrow*, she told herself, *I'll buy a dog whistle for Bally, and never call his name out loud again.*

Chapter four.

The bell in the church tower clanged out seven times, and as if summoned, dusk crept into the graveyard soon afterwards. A man sagged against a sarcophagus, sucked the last of the flesh from an overripe plum, and then aimed the stone at the cause of all his trouble. From just outside the church's wrought iron gates, Balkind cackled his annoyance and rattled his wings in warning, but made no move to enter.

'We have to go home!' the Rider told him. 'This is not our world.'

Balkind ducked his head and did his best impression of a beaten and cowed griffin, but still refused to budge.

The Rider sighed. Even if he could persuade the creature into the graveyard, this didn't feel right, not any more. Earlier, the mist had glimmered with a supernatural sheen and a strong smell of burning charcoal filled the air, conveying a sense of – not *déjà vu*, but of destiny. Still, he tried again:

'Balkind, come – this might be our last chance.'

But the obstinate creature merely waddled backwards. Then, with a mournful bellow, he swung his head, indicating the direction in which the girl had recently stomped away.

His rider frowned. Balkind was considered "difficult" even by the griffin master. As an expendable nobody, he had been chosen to ride the pig-headed youngster, although sometimes the thought crossed his mind that Balkind had chosen *him*. Six years of working as the griffin master's serf in return for food and lodging had finally paid off. The Rider had learned to ignore the dirty looks and mutterings, and even worse, the snubs from the other recruits. To climb on Balkind's back and soar effortlessly through the skies made up for being an outcast. Sometimes, ducking his head alongside Balkind's neck and riding the thermals far above people scurrying about the ground like insects, he *became* part of the griffin, and the griffin an extension of him. So when Balkind wandered off into this strange other world, he had followed.

'I don't blame you for wanting to stay here.' He said out loud. 'But we have a duty to get back. Besides – I don't think there are many lady griffins in this world.'

The stone the Rider leaned against leaked the last of the autumn sun's heat, and a chill entered his back. He'd been shocked to realise that each of these markers indicated where a dead body lay. In his world, once a spirit had departed, its flesh was cremated, so no magician could make use of the empty shell. These markers had strange carvings, which appeared to follow a pattern. He guessed them to be a form of writing, probably names, to enable the body markers to be identified.

I should have a name, he mused, and began running several through his mind.

Growing up, he had believed his name to be "Clear-Off", the phrase men ducking into his mother's hut had greeted him with. Then the griffin master had plucked him from the rabble of snot nosed kids roaming the streets, and his name changed to "boy". The other recruits referred to him as "Balkind's Rider" when Romulus was in earshot. Otherwise he was "Whore's-Son", never to his face of course, not after that one incident...

The Rider swallowed against the bad taste in his mouth. That last plum must have been sour, he reasoned; it had certainly done nothing to fill the emptiness inside him.

He felt loath to leave this sanctuary, but unwilling to raid the containers where these other-worlders dumped perfectly good bones with their waste. Not that he relished the taste of raw marrow. His stomach cramped at the memory. If they were trapped here, he would have to find food, and somewhere better to shelter. From the brow of the meadow, he'd spotted a wooden barn. With luck the newly mown hay would be stored there. If they went now, they might even stand a chance of surprising a rabbit or two along the way. A light drizzle began to fall, and that decided him.

'Come on, Balkind.'

The griffin's ears pricked forward, and a clucking noise – his "happy sound" – started up in his throat.

'No, not that way.' With any luck once Balkind had a full stomach and a night's sleep the bird-brained creature would forget this strange attachment he imagined he had with the red haired girl.

The Rider sighed heavily again. He reached up, grabbed Balkind's sensitive snout and twisted.

'This way.' He said firmly. He strode out of the copse and started up the meadow. Balkind lumbered alongside, between him and the overhanging canopy of trees.

Even the Rider could barely make out the griffin's shadowy form. Twice it made a quick darting movement; then came a squeal followed by a crunching of small bones. The Rider's stomach churned again at the thought of digesting raw marrow, and at the same time complained of its emptiness. The Rider tried not to think of the last time he'd eaten properly, and then tried not to think of eating at all. Then he scolded himself mentally. *"Look on this as a training exercise – first objective – survival!"* Romulus of course, had lectured his recruits on what to do if ever stranded in enemy territory.

'Act natural and blend in,' he had said (this had caused much laughter, the thought of the battle-scarred Romulus blending in anywhere) and 'Take what you need. It isn't stealing – it's booty.'

This the Rider had done – to an extent. The rucksack had been dumped on top of a pile of rotting vegetation to one side of the church wall, obviously unwanted. And it had been simple enough to liberate some short trousers and a cotton vest pegged to a line in a nearby garden. But stealing food might prove more difficult.

He pondered this problem as they neared the barn. At least he wouldn't have to break into the building: he saw that one side of the large wooden structure was completely open. On seeing neat stacks of oblong hay bales filling one half of the barn, the Rider felt relieved. Within a short time, he'd fashioned a griffin-sized cave from some of the bales, then, after a struggle, ripped a couple of bales open and scattered hay over Balkind who snuffled at it, grateful to be finally receiving the care and attention a griffin deserved. He grunted when the Rider snuggled up under one of his wings, but didn't fidget or try to shrug him off. Tomorrow he would be forced to steal again. But for tonight, they would be warm and dry; and one of them, at least, would have a full stomach. Closing his eyes, a vision of the girl rose in his mind. With her red hair and milky white skin, she reminded him of strawberries and cream. He smiled, thinking that was a good description; fresh sweet strawberries with a hint of tartness, and a soft centre.

<<<<<*****>>>>>

He hadn't been dreaming, he wasn't dreaming: a screaming had awoken him, and Balkind was no longer at his back. Once he was sure of that, he snatched up his rucksack and jumped to his feet. A wave of nausea and dizziness swept over him. He swayed as he took deep breaths and tried to regain his senses. Screams ripped through the night again, the hysterical screams of a woman. Still disoriented, the Rider took off down the meadow, heading towards the dark outline of a hedge. The screams were coming from the field on the other side, and he could make out words now.

'Get off me! Get off me!' A wordless screech followed and then 'Help! Help!'

The Rider raced along the hedge, searching for a way through hawthorn bushes and finding none, hurled himself headfirst into the leafy branches, pushing past the spiteful thorns and brambles that tore at his skin in a thousand places.

Having regained his feet, the Rider started forward again, but something tugged back, tightening its grip around his ankles and he toppled over, crashing headlong into a rough grass and thistle covered field. He twisted around; it seemed he'd stumbled across a strand of metal. When he tried to kick free, tiny prongs lacerated his skin. The screaming stopped abruptly, but screams from another throat began almost immediately. Cursing his own clumsiness, the Rider twisted to unravel the thin strand of silvery metal caught up around his ankles, biting his lip when the wire's prongs snagged at his hands. When he sat up he saw that people were moving around at the bottom end of the field, if he could extricate himself quickly, he might still be able to halt this bedlam.

At last the Rider freed his legs from the wire that seared his skin. He rolled over onto his back, and shouted at the top of his voice:

"Balkind! Drop!"

Chapter five.

Instead of telling Bally off, Frankie's mum greeted him like the return of the prodigal son. He even had chicken for dinner. Tony pulled a face, but didn't say anything. He'd learned never to criticise anything concerning Michael or Michael's dog a long time ago.

The usual Friday night stuff happened, Tony left for work, and Frankie and her mum got stuck into tidying the house.

'Thanks for picking Bally up love. Did school give you any trouble?'

They were on the last stage of clearing away dinner, mum washing up, Frankie drying up. She rubbed the inside of a glass vigorously, making sure there were no water stains before putting it into the cupboard, thinking it wasn't school that gave her trouble.

'Not really mum.' And a longing to know if her real trouble had made it home struck Frankie. 'I've got to go round Annette's though – pick up some homework.'

Mum was immediately defensive. 'The phone hasn't rung.'

'She emailed me.' Thanks to mum, Frankie didn't have a mobile. She used to have one, in fact she'd had several, but school kept confiscating them. Mainly because of mum texting her several times a day to make certain she wasn't dead. Frankie had overheard Tony and mum arguing about this once. Mum had cried, and promised she'd stop smothering her daughter, but still Frankie *knew* she was the only fifteen year old in the country not allowed out after dark without a good excuse.

'Lightning doesn't strike in the same place twice.' Tony had shouted at mum, and she'd agreed. Frankie wanted to tell them that statistically it *does* strike twice, and sometimes even three times in the same place. But she didn't, and hoped for more freedom, but it never happened.

'Make sure you call me when you get there.'

Frankie sighed heavily. 'Her phone isn't working mum. That's why she emailed me.' Her tone implied she'd already told her mum this, and only had to remind her because her mum was old and growing forgetful.

After showering, Frankie threw on a dark grey tracksuit— a cheap designer knock-off, consoling herself that it was dark and no one would see her. She was just about to slip out the front door when a thought occurred to her. Entering the front room, she saw her mum had already donned pyjamas, and was slumped on the couch, with Bally laying over her legs.

Frankie scuttled between her mum and the telly to pick up her X-Box controller without making a sound. But Bally lifted his head, her mum stirred, and sat up.

'What do you need that for?' *Christ*, Frankie thought, *every time I go out – an interrogation!*

'We might play a bit of X-Box,' she said glibly. Her mum sniffed. After dropping a kiss on her forehead, and telling Bally to settle back down, Frankie left the house.

Instead of crossing the road and cutting across the common, which was asking for trouble with all the poaching that had been going on recently, Frankie walked along the pavement for half a mile or so, then crossed the main road. Chestnut trees lined the length of the drive leading to the church, and experience had taught her to walk in the middle of the road, especially during autumn.

The drive culminated in a turning circle at the church gates, and Frankie stepped off asphalt onto the footpath running between Six Acre Meadow, and the church wall. It was slippery underfoot. People weren't supposed to, but they tossed wilted flowers and stagnant vase water over the wall rather than carry them back to the compost heap. Ahead of her the woods loomed, and Frankie's vision grew dimmer. She used the church wall as a handrail.

Michael had been walking along this very wall when it happened. He'd been showing off, practising base jumping, and back-flipping, landing on his feet. After one such flip, Chelsi, the stupid mare, had clapped out loud, and Frankie's brother had looked back over his shoulder and lost his balance. As he fell, he clipped his temple against a headstone.

"Rest in Peace. Mary Howland 1845 – 1910. She was a gentlewoman." Frankie wanted to scream at the irony every time she passed this way. A dead gentlewoman had killed her brother – but not outright – that was the one ray of hope. 'He's not dead yet!' Frankie muttered to herself, automatically.

The shaped stone under her hand which capped the top of the wall was called coping. Frankie knew this stuff because of her architect dad. Or rather her ex-architect dad. Shortly after Michael was moved from the specialist neurological department at Charring Cross hospital to a nursing home on the Essex coast, Frankie's dad had upped sticks and immigrated to Spain, where he took up painting landscapes. Every time Michael got an infection, the nursing home called her mum, to confirm that she still wanted Michael to be resuscitated. This was because Frankie's dad had given instructions for him *not* to be resuscitated. Frankie knew all this because she'd sneaked a look at Michael's notes once.

"DNR?/Check with mother", was the mystifying phrase scribbled in red ink across the beige folder containing Michael's case history.

Frankie had waited for Monday to ask the school nurse what the abbreviation meant. The nurse gave a garbled explanation, and scuttled off before she could be thanked. Frankie watched her go thinking "Yeah well, I suppose filing paperwork is pretty important."

'But that was years ago, and in another country.' Frankie said out loud, climbing over the stile that lead to the swampy bottom part of the woods. It was even darker among the trees, but the path widened. Someone had festooned one of the giant chestnuts with wide blue ribbon, and tacked a blue football shirt with a handwritten poem dedicated to "Grand-dad" underneath, and left some chrysanthemums at the tree's base. This kind of "pagan behaviour" inflamed the vicar, but despite his ranting and raving, he never managed to catch the culprits.

Frankie squelched along the rabbits' track that circled the swamp, and immediately saw her quest had been in vain. The only indication that a large creature had rested here was an absence of complete darkness where brambles and undergrowth should be, and a saddle patch of luminous moss missing from the fallen log Balkind's owner had sat on to wait for dusk. Frankie waited to be sure, unwilling to call out, uncertain of what might answer her.

Shadows flickered and shimmered on the edges of her vision, and every time she got a fix on one, another would move. Frankie knew it was only her mind playing tricks as her eyes strained to focus into the darkness, and she *knew* the rustling of the undergrowth was caused by rabbits, or maybe rats scurrying about their nightly business. And of course Frankie knew it was only an overactive imagination, but in the quietness, it seemed that listeners waited in the shadows, straining to hear her voice. Frankie's nerve broke, and she forged towards the blandness of the meadow, keeping well clear of the swamp, uncaring of the brambles catching at her legs. Behind her, the darkness settled again, and she leapt into the openness of the meadow where the only shadow was her own. Street lights from the village centre beckoned to Frankie from the left, about a mile or so away.

'It's Friday night, and I deserve *some* fun!' Frankie said out loud. Annette's house could be reached in ten minutes or so by trekking across country, and she'd already braved the darkest part of the common.

'So long as I don't run into any dragons this time, I'll be fine.'

Ignoring the voice that sounded like her mum's warning her not to wander the countryside at night, Frankie set off to see her friend.

Chapter six.

Frankie vaulted into a field where cows grazed during the day. The meadow's pale stubble had somehow created an illusion of light, and now what little night vision she'd acquired instantly vanished. But this field, though dark, was only the length of a football pitch. *I'll walk home along the main road*, Frankie told herself. With high careful steps, she began making her way across the field, towards the stile and the alleyway leading to Annette's street, hoping her trainers didn't land in a cowpat.

She'd been walking for less than a minute when, without warning, a brilliant flash lit up the whole area. Blinking, Frankie shielded her eyes, *what on earth?!*

Then she realized what it was; and felt relief, followed immediately by annoyance. Poachers! Someone was out "lamping": Small creatures, such as rabbits, would automatically freeze under a bright light, making an easy target for anyone with a shot-gun. Frankie wished again she had a mobile; she'd report them like a shot.

Then she realised whoever was behind that flashlight could see *her*, and they had a gun. She tried to hurry without actually running towards the stile, trying to act nonchalantly, but the other side of the "football field" now seemed at least a mile away. *They're poaching, and probably more worried about you than you are them*, she told herself, but the tightness in her chest remained, and Frankie wished she'd just gone straight home.

The light flicked off again, causing Frankie to stumble and fall to the ground. Even as she put out her hands to save herself, she heard the "crazy frog" buzz of two mopeds. A second later she was blinded again – by headlights this time – and an angry buzzing of engines reverberated through the rough ground as they passed.

Frankie got up and ran for the stile, but one of the mopeds circled around and cut off her escape. Whirling, she screamed at the top of her lungs and ran the other way, still blinded from the light, straight into the arms of Pete Roberts.

Frankie still couldn't see too well, but knew it was him, by the crew cut hair and sticky out ears and smell of cheap cologne. He grabbed Frankie's hands, pulling her against him, twisting her round.

'Not so tough now are you? I'll teach you to knock my little brother flying, you clumsy cow!' Then he lashed out with his foot and knocked Frankie's legs from under her.

Frankie crashed to the ground full length, and let out an 'ooffff!' as Pete's body landed on top of her. Frankie spat into his face, then screamed again for help, loudly enough to wake the dead. Over Pete's shoulder, Frankie saw the second moped flying towards them. Its brakes squealed and the engine died with a rattle. Its rider dismounted, allowing the moped to crash to the ground, and Frankie's heart sank even farther. Jason Beech was only half Pete's height, but twice as nasty. He drew back his foot and kicked the struggling girl in the ribs. Frankie's chest hurt, but she managed to scream again.

'Shut your stupid mouth, you stupid ginger minger.' Jason stooped and tore off his trainer, and then his sock, which he stuffed into Frankie's mouth.

Gagging, she spat it out and shouted: 'Help! Help!'

Jason grabbed a handful of Frankie's hair, yanking her head back, and stuffed the sock into her mouth again. This time Frankie couldn't spit it out. She choked. Her palms stung where she'd fallen over, her scalp was on fire, but far far worse, Pete's knee jabbed firmly against her stomach. He kept Frankie pinned down while Jason rummaged through his pockets, and with a cry of delight, produced a knife, which he passed to a grinning Pete. 'I'm gonna scalp me a redhead!' he leered, twisting the handful of hair he held in his left hand, and pulling it taunt. With a frantic motion, Frankie jerked her head away, pulling her hair from his grasp. Pete struck her forehead with the heel of his hand, and cursing, folded the knife and tucked it through his belt, and began gathering her hair into a twist again, this time using both hands to make certain he caught up every last tendril.

Frankie's blood pounded, and her eyes bulged, unable to look away from the matt black handle and sliver of blade with its wicked serrations jammed through Pete's belt. This couldn't be happening! *Stupid stupid stupid!* Sneaking out from home – no-one would ever believe she hadn't come here of her own free will; Pete and Jason would laugh it off as a prank that got out of hand. She swivelled her head, to see what Jason was doing. With one hand slung casually across Frankie's mouth to keep the sock in place, he juggled his mobile in the other. He sniggered as he gazed at the tiny screen, and for the briefest moment, relaxed the pressure against Frankie's mouth. With a frantic last gasp action, she scrunched some of the sock aside with her tongue, and chomped down hard, crushing two of Jason's fingers between her teeth, biting through flesh and into bone.

'Bitch!' He shrilled, snatching his hand away. Frankie rocked her body upwards and butted her head against Pete's chin. He arched backwards, putting out an arm to stop himself falling, and his body weight lifted from her. Frankie scrambled out from under him, staggered to her feet, and ran for her life.

She almost made it. She'd almost reached the main road when fingers snarled her hair and Pete captured her again.

Frankie knew she'd never get away a second time. Sobbing helplessly, she closed her eyes and tried to pretend she wasn't really there, and this wasn't really happening. Pete slapped at her head, her shoulders—his open palms seemed to be everywhere—and Frankie rocked backwards and forwards, trying to lessen the force of his blows.

'You almost bit his finger off!' he screamed into her face. Jason stumbled up, bent almost double, nursing his hand against his body.

'Let me at her!' he growled. 'I'll teach her not to ...'

His voice was drowned out by a roar. Frankie's insides clenched at the sound. It was bestial, and seemed to come from all around; from everywhere. All three teenagers started. Pete was the first to look up. Frankie followed his gaze. There, hanging in the sky, was a dark presence. It blotted out what little light there was, and its wings were as large as sail cloths. Then, with a thunderclap, the creature's wings flapped, and it headed straight towards the three teenagers.

Jason forgot to nurse his hand. 'What ... what ... ?' he stammered.

With a cry of panic, Pete took off – he simply ran. Jason snarled, and then lost his nerve too. He tried to crouch behind Frankie, angling her body towards the demon that skimmed over the field, with great shiny talons outstretched. A blast of humid air streamed Frankie's hair upwards and outwards, and she cheered as Balkind flapped past. The griffin snatched at Pete's legs, and carried him into the air as easily as an eagle would swipe up a mouse. Frankie cheered again as Pete screamed, dangling upside-down from Balkind's talons. Behind her, Jason whimpered, and clutched at her ankle. Frankie kicked his hand away.

Then, because someone always has to come along and spoil the fun, a voice shouted: 'Balkind – drop!'

The griffin faltered, banked slightly to fly over the church's tower, and let go. Pete Roberts fell, tumbling end-over-end for several seconds before crashing to earth among the canopy of trees that bordered the graveyard. Frankie hoped he'd landed in the swamp.

'Yes!' Frankie jumped for joy, punching the air. 'Way to go Balkind!'

Then she turned to grin at Jason, whose face was slack and stupid—even more so than usual. Gibbering with terror, he turned and ran. Not towards his friend, but in the opposite direction from Balkind.

Fifty feet above Frankie, an odd clucking noise came from Balkind's throat, as he carved a semi-circle in the air. Seconds later, he landed and gambolled over. Frankie half expected him to stick his tongue out and try to lick her face. She wouldn't have minded, just that one time. Frankie hugged his neck, Balkind's head rested against her shoulder, and she stroked and petted the giant beast.

'Good boy, oh good boy, oh good good boy.'

From the corner of her eye, Frankie saw the Rider approaching, limping and looking as though he'd been dragged through a hedge backwards. It was too dark to see his expression, but if his body language was anything to go by, the Rider was furious.

Balkind saw him too, and with a last nuzzle of Frankie's ear, crouched down as though trying to make himself invisible. Frankie could see the Rider's face now – and yep! He was almost beside himself with rage. His bare arms and legs were covered with small welts, and mud spattered his hair and tee-shirt.

Becoming aware of Frankie for the first time, he stopped in his tracks, and stared. He reached forward and tugged at something in her hair, retrieving a handful of twigs.

'What happened to you?' They spoke together.

He stepped closer, and stroked Frankie's hair back over her shoulder.

'What are you doing here anyway?' he said. Some of the fierceness returned to his face. He glanced over toward the church, where Balkind had dumped Pete Roberts, and put two and two together. When he looked back at Frankie, his face had softened again. 'Little girl, you shouldn't be out here all on your own.'

The sympathy in his voice broke her. Frankie put her head in her hands, sunk to her knees on the grass, and sobbed.

Chapter seven.

"And then this dragon swooped down and grabbed me with its claws. It flew me over the meadow and dumped me in the swamp."
Perched on the edge of a pale green armless easy chair, Special Police Constable Lee Haines dutifully copied the boy's words into his notebook.

'You can wipe that sneer off your face young man, you're only one of them specials. My son's not ...' Peter Roberts Senior broke off at that point, and Haines wondered whether the next word was to have been "mad" or "drunk."
'What my husband means is that our son isn't prone to inventing things,' added Mrs Roberts.
As Haines looked at the scion of the house, who was at that moment wedged between his overweight parents on a matching pale green leather sofa, he tended to believe the mother. Her son claimed to be sixteen, but looked closer to twenty, and had "yob" written all over him, from the razor cuts in his cropped hair to the tightly laced Dr Martin "Bovva Boy" boots.
'Are you certain you didn't just have a nasty tumble?' Haines asked, in a sympathetic tone he normally reserved for small children and elderly ladies.

Peter Roberts Senior sat back, crossed his arms, and fixed the young "Special" with a stare. Then he turned to the boy.
'Show him son. Show him where the dragon clawed you.'
The kid stood up and wriggled out of his tee-shirt. 'Those are very nasty marks,' said Haines.
'Nasty marks! You bleeding idiot – a whopping great dragon picked him up and flew with him over the hill!'
'We've just come back from the hospital,' said the mother. 'The doctors said they'd never seen anything like these marks.'
Haines had never *heard* anything like this story. He felt his mouth twist in disbelief.
'If you're going to sit there taking the mickey, you can get out now!' shouted Roberts. 'Tell the cop shop I wanna proper policeman – not one of the part timers.'

'I'm sorry sir,' said Haines, 'but I'm afraid all our dragon specialists are tied up at present. I'll just take a few snaps of your son's – dragon wounds – and maybe he can give me a full description of his assailant? We'll get an identi-kit made up.'

Peter Roberts Senior simmered as his son was photographed front and rear, and then, too enthusiastically for his liking, gave a description of the dragon which had appeared "like a demon from hell".

He glared at his wife, stroking the back of his son's neck, and urging him to be brave, and wished to hell they hadn't called the police, or, for that matter, troubled the local accident and emergency department. The casualty nurse had seemed especially interested in details, almost as though she too was compiling a report. But when his son had burst into the house earlier, wild eyed and trembling uncontrollably, his story seemed to have the ring of truth to it. For the past two hours, he, Peter Roberts, at forty-five the owner of a successful construction company, and himself built like a brick out-house, had believed in dragons.

Bloody hell, I hope this doesn't get out, he thought. *I'll be the laughing stock of the country.* Then he glanced across at the special constable, who met his gaze with a wink, and Peter Roberts Senior's heart sank to the bottom of his steel toe capped boots.

The police radio crackled to life, and Haines twisted the radio to his mouth, to acknowledge the call. Then he stood and walked across the polished wooden floorboards to the far end of the spacious living room.

Mrs Roberts continued to murmur comfortingly to their son; Peter Roberts waved her to silence. He wanted to ear-wig in. As he watched, he saw the smarmy young constable's back straighten, as he practically stood to attention.

'Yes sir,' he was saying. 'I understand sir, I'm just with the victim's family now. The young man appears very shaken, a very nasty incident indeed sir.' Then, after a pause, 'Yes sir, I understand. My full report will be on the chief's desk within the hour.'

Clicking off his radio, he turned back into the room. Gone was the mocking manner, Roberts noticed: the officer was all efficiency now.

'It appears we have photographic evidence of the incident,' said Haines, 'and a special investigation will begin as soon as we've interviewed everyone.' He flicked back through his notebook, then looked directly at the boy.

'Can you give me the names of everyone who you know, or suspect might have witnessed your attack?'

'Oh you've got photographic evidence and suddenly you believe our son?' jeered the wife.

'I keep an open mind madam.' SPC Haines flumped back down in his seat, and the armchair let out a small huff of air. With his pen poised, he flicked over to a blank page in his notebook.

'Now, once more, young man, and this time I want to know *exactly* what you were up to on that common, and I want the names of everyone present.'

Twenty-five minutes later, Special Constable Haines left, warning the Roberts family not to speak to any members of the press. Immediately Pete Roberts junior and Mrs Roberts started jabbering together.

'Wow dad! Do you think this'll get on telly? – I could be famous!'

'Well, he certainly changed his tune a bit quick – you could see he didn't believe our Pete, then all of a sudden – he did believe!' Pam Roberts darted over to the house phone adding 'Wait till I tell our Sandra!'

'Dad – do you think I'll be famous?!' Pete asked again anxiously.

Shaking his head, Peter Roberts hurried across the room to intercept his wife, snatching the phone from her hands and slamming it down into its receiver.

'You're not calling anyone!' he shouted. 'And you shut up, Pete! You've caused enough bloody upheaval tonight. You stay away from that common, and you – ' He turned to his wife— 'keep your trap shut as well! Understand? Something weird is going on up at that common, and I don't know what to believe – but I know one thing – it's unnatural.'

Despite the central heating being on full blast, all three of them shivered at his words.

'You're right dad, let the police deal with it now.'

Pam Roberts nodded: 'Let the police deal with it,' she echoed, adding 'I hope they shoot the damn thing, and send it straight back to hell!'

Chapter eight.

Two prominent veins, fringed with feathers, ran either side along the top outline of Balkind's shoulder blades. When Frankie cupped her hand over one, it throbbed against her palm. She traced the vein with her hand, and Balkind shivered. Her hand travelled along the vein, which measured her arm's length, before folding back on itself. When she thrust her fingers between the fold, she felt a soft leathery skin, which also pulsed; it must have its own network of minor veins. The major artery folded back on itself several times, and Frankie estimated that when fully outstretched, Balkind's wing span would be around thirty feet from wing tip to wing tip.

'What happens if you fall off?'

'You pray your griffin catches you before you hit the ground.'

Frankie's head jerked around to look over at the Rider, sprawled on the sofa bed, across the shack from her. With sirens blaring in their ears, they'd hurried along the service road running behind the length Frankie's street, and snuck into her rear garden. Then Frankie had doubled back into her house, and called to mum that she'd be in the shack for the next hour or two, practising her piano scales. She raided the fridge, then raided the medicine cabinet, and twenty minutes later, the shack reeked of TCP antiseptic. Now Frankie felt her nerves beginning to calm, as she played her hands along the griffin's wings. Balkind's eyes were semi-closed, and he crooned with the happiness of a griffin who had feasted on three tins of best quality dog's meat. She could only offer the Rider left-over chicken drumsticks and some cheese sandwiches, but it appeared they were satisfactory. At least, judging from the empty plates stacked on the old kitchen table, alongside a digital piano keyboard.

Now Frankie stared at him, but apart from a mocking look in his eyes, the Rider's face was expressionless. She forced a smile: 'Was that another "silly question?"'

The Rider glanced up at the ceiling, as though to say "give me strength" and Frankie just knew he found all her questions "silly."

'At least I don't have to ask what a service road is – or a car!'

The Rider frowned, and Frankie arched her eyebrows mockingly, widening her eyes. Raising her hand, she rubbed Balkind's shoulder in the exact spot the Rider stroked him. Balkind responded by collapsing his knees and crouching down, and Frankie swallowed a gasp of surprise. Smirking at the Rider, she sat down close to Balkind, crossed her legs, and pulled the griffin's head into her lap.

'Tell you what. I'll ask you five "silly" questions, and you can ask me five "silly" questions.'

The Rider's frown deepened. 'But how do I know if they're silly or not?'

Frankie couldn't help herself. 'Ask yourself the question again, only slower,' she taunted. Ducking his head, the Rider glowered at her, and then the corners of his lips tugged up into a smile. Frankie wanted to tell him that he really needed to work on his sense of humour, but didn't. The Rider came from another universe, one in which fun seemed to have been outlawed. An air of expectancy swelled inside the dimness of the shack.

'Who goes first?' The Rider finally broke the silence.

'Was that your first question?' Frankie teased, and then giggled when he retorted 'was that your first question?' Cradling Balkind's head with one arm, she stretched out with the other towards a stray tennis ball, and chucked it in the Rider's direction. He dodged, caught it and chucked it back. 'You've got quite a good aim, for a girl.' He said, as Balkind snuffled at the tennis ball, as though trying to determine if it were edible or not. Frankie raised her eyebrows again, wrinkling her nose for good measure, and a question arrived in her mind. Without thinking, she blurted it out: 'What will you do if you can't get home?'

The Rider stilled. He rested his elbows on his knees, then steepled his long fingers together, and rested his chin on his hands. His eyes focused on something very far away, as he considered what his options might be if he couldn't return home.

Frankie squirmed, 'I'm sorry, I didn't mean – look, you ask me a question now – you don't have to answer that one,' she stammered. The Rider shook himself, and stood up. He walked over to the wall opposite to the one Frankie leaned against, and peered at a map of the British Isles. 'Is this Albion?' he asked. Frankie wrinkled her brow, and with a last stroke of Balkind's head, moved it gently from her lap to the floorboards, and stood up.

'That's a map of this country.' She said, stalking over in bare feet to stand beside him, and tilting her head to look at the familiar landmass. She'd given it to Michael on their twelfth birthday, when he was still obsessed with collecting different minerals and relics from the past. 'It shows all the ancient settlements – where artefacts are likely to be found. See – here's Stonehenge – this here is–'

'–Glastonbury Tor' the Rider interrupted. 'And the Wessex ley-line runs from here–' his fingers scythed across the map, brushing from Dorset, through Stonehenge across to London '–to here.'

'The Wessex what what?' Frankie asked, standing on tiptoes to peer closer at the map. 'That's not one of my questions by the way.'

'Sounded like two to me.' The Rider peeled the map from the wall, and casting a glance around the room, walked over to place the map on the kitchen table, moving the empty plates and digital piano keyboard to the floor. Then he pulled the makeshift desk over to the sofa and sat down, patting the cushion beside him, inviting Frankie to take a seat. 'Make yourself at home, why don't you?' Frankie muttered, as she sat down next to him.

'Third question.' The Rider told her, smoothing the map over the desk. Frankie wanted to say "fourth actually," but kept quiet, and kept her advantage. Balkind lifted his head to peer at the sofa, and seeing nothing edible, or of interest to griffins, slumped his chin back to the ground with a grunt.

The Rider placed a thumb over the River Thames. 'Is this London?' he asked. Frankie jogged his hand a little 'here's London, and we're here – ' someone had scrawled "Leybridge" with an arrow pointing to the village. On the map, it barely featured, although there was a small marker for the old church. But otherwise the area was puddled with blue, representing the lakes, and green fields.

The Rider pointed to a section of contours, denoting hills, about three inches above Leybridge village, or in real life, thirty miles. 'Are these hills or mountains?' He asked.

Frankie looked, and underlined the words written along the swathe of brown with her fingernail: 'Chiltern Hills,' she read out loud. 'Can't you read?' she added.

'Yes, of course I can, and that's your last question.' The Rider snapped. Frankie didn't know if he were joking or not, or if she'd made him angry (again) or if he were just concentrating on the map.

'In my world, Ella-Earth, this is called Albion.' He swept his hand over the map again. 'And these hills are mountains, and there's a lot more water.' He mused for a moment or two. 'There are caves in the Delphia mountains – what you call Chiltern Hills.'

'And you think they might make a good place to hide a griffin,' Frankie guessed.

He shrugged, and then looked directly at her. 'Are there caves in the Chiltern Hills?' She nodded slowly, 'yes, there's a very famous cave there – ' For some reason, her dad had loved that place, and often taken her and Michael for outings to the Devil's Hell Fire Club. Frankie didn't like it there much – Regency Rakes such as Lord Byron and his friends were reputed to have really lived it up – even enlarging caves and carving out new tunnels. But now the tunnels and caves were empty, and to her mind, boring, damp and chilly. The Rider was studying the map again, as though trying to memorise landmarks. 'You can have that if you like,' Frankie said. The Rider shot her a quick glance, and then nodded his thanks, and began furling the map up.

'Wait – you haven't explained "leydo" lines to me.' Frankie placed her hand on his, and with a sigh, the Rider unrolled the map and spread it out over the desk again.

Marking sections off the map with quick sweeps of his hand, the Rider began a garbled explanation: 'There are four major ley-lines, North, East, South and West.' Frankie frowned – 'No – this is North, East, South and West' The Rider had counted off the compass points from the bottom of the map, she counted them from the top. The Rider screwed his eyes shut tightly, and grimaced. 'Ugh, no wonder ....' Opening his eyes he jabbed a finger towards Scotland. 'This is your North?'

Frankie nodded, 'Does this mean you've been trying to get home in the wrong direction?' The Rider made a rocking motion with his hand. 'It wouldn't make any difference – it shouldn't make any difference.' He traced an imaginary line from Glastonbury Tor, up through Dorset and through London and into Leybridge and beyond to Oxfordshire. Frankie saw that Leybridge stood in direct alignment with six major landmarks, including Glastonbury Tor, Stonehenge, and the Tower of London, with a dozen or so smaller marks to indicate that monoliths – or standing stones –were scattered along the way.

'That's a ley-line?'

The Rider nodded, and traced three similar lines, 'The Northern Connection, The Sussex Way, and The Eastern Approach.' He dropped his gaze to stare at the Wessex Ley-line again, and there was a longing in his eyes.

Frankie reached up, and put an arm around his shoulders, they felt tense and rigid. 'You'll get back home, I'm sure you'll find a way.' He slumped momentarily, and then they both started as a voice called out 'Frankie – what are you doing out there? Come inside – I want to lock the back door.'

Balkind's ears pricked, but otherwise he didn't stir. With a quick squeeze of the Rider's shoulders, Frankie rose, and walked over to the shack's door. Opening it an inch or two she called back – 'Five more minutes mum, I'm just trying to memorise these last chords.'

Balkind's big green eyes followed Frankie as she walked back to the sofa. 'I've got to go – there's a duvet and pillows under the cushions.' When he looked at her blankly, she huffed and motioned him to get up. Then she began pulling off cushions, and retrieving the pillows, laid them at one end of the sofa, and shook the duvet out over the sofa's main frame. The Rider blinked in surprise. 'Thank you,' he said stiffly. 'No worries,' Frankie replied, with a shrug. Then she frowned, he hadn't answered her question, not really. 'So what's the big deal with these ley-lines?'

The Rider grimaced, motioning to the map he said 'Powerful magnetic currents run along the ley-lines. These monoliths and other stone structures act as neutralisers – or 'earthers'. Without this balance, or checks – '

A shrill voice interrupted him: ' – Frankie – come in now!'

'Alright mum! I'm coming!' She spun round to the Rider again – 'Without these balances or checks – go on –'

'The forces would be uncontrolled – any sudden surge would result in our two universes colliding. Before we,' he placed a hand on his own chest, and indicated Frankie to include the inhabitants of both universes, 'before we discovered how to keep the forces in check, there was a lot more interaction between our two worlds.'

'But – that sounds really cool!' Frankie's eyes shone at the thought. The Rider grimaced again. 'It might sound "cool", but when men came from this world, to our Ella-Earth, their first action was to slaughter our wise men.' His eyes darkened, and his mouth narrowed to a thin line.

'But why?'

'Because they wanted to impose their own wise men on us. But their wisdom and ways are not our ways, and seem not wise to us. They call themselves "The Elite." We call them "The Uninvited".' Something in his tone caused Frankie to shiver involuntarily.

'And when I called out – I was inviting Balkind?' Frankie whispered, alarmed at the anger on his face.

He shrugged, 'How should I know what goes on in a griffin's mind?' His features softened slightly. 'I forget, you're only a little girl; yes it appears you created a way for Balkind, and his rider to cross through the membrane that separates our two worlds.'

'And now you're stuck here.' Frankie stated, ignoring the "little girl" jibe.

'There's still hope. On Ella-Earth, four noblemen, four lords of the ley-lines are guardians of the stones. They each possess a crystal, which has the power to neutralise the neutralisers, if you want.' He thought for a moment or two, before adding 'And there is also another crystal: "The Ella-Stone" – a crystal powerful enough to control all four ley-lines; but some think that is just a myth.'

'Frankie – when I find my slippers – I'm coming out there!' A scratching at the door announced Bally was already outside, in the garden, and Frankie prayed he didn't bark. 'Two seconds, mum!' Frankie called back.

'But the crystals – the ley-lines – they're on Ella-Earth.' Her stomach flipped over at the thought.

The Rider cupped her elbow, and walked her over to the door. 'Have you not been listening to me? This world is my world's twin. Have you never stood on any of those paths,' he threw a hand over to the map, 'and felt a distant throbbing? Besides – Lord Leifur, the guardian of the Wessex ley-line, vanished to this world, over fifteen years ago. I know at least one of those crystals is here, in this world.' Frankie's gaze fell upon Michael's collection of rocks arranged on a honeycomb shelf hanging on the shack's wall. The Rider followed her gaze, and uttered a brief laugh. It sounded like a sob. 'I wish it were that simple.' Opening the door, he ushered her out into the garden, dropping a hand on Bally's enquiring nose. 'Now go, and sweet dreams, and thank you.'

Chapter nine.

The tinkling chimes of her mum's mobile woke Frankie up. It was just one beat off "get out of bed, it's a beautiful day." She listened to it, trying to make the words sit on the notes, waiting for it to ring itself out, and two thoughts swarmed into her consciousness: Mum wasn't around to turn the alarm off; she normally woke at the sound of a feather dropping, and either her own alarm hadn't gone off, or she'd slept through it – again.

Frankie stared blearily at the old fashioned radio alarm sitting on her bedside cabinet, running last night over in her mind. Especially worrying were the police and ambulance sirens that had started up halfway through the nerve-wracking journey home. When seven-zero-four finally focused in red neon digits, Frankie saw that the alarm had been set for six pm, rather than six am. Mum had probably woken before her alarm went off, and taken Bally out for his early morning walk. If she hurried, there'd be time to slosh some milk over a bowl of cornflakes, and sneak out a couple of tins of dog food into the garden shack.

Frankie glanced out of the window as she pulled on her second best jeans, watching as a car crawled along waterlogged tarmac. The driver veered onto the wrong side of the road to avoid the pond which had formed overnight almost outside Frankie's house. It must have rained heavily in the night, and the clouds threatened more rain; so much for the "beautiful day", she thought. More to the point, her mum was probably walking Bally over the park, rather than the common and would be home at any moment.

Rushing now, Frankie shoved her arms into a tee-shirt, tugged it over her head, then shrugged on a track suit top and bounded down the stairs, freeing her hair from inside the tee-shirt and track top as she went. A short sharp metallic rat-a-tat tat at the front door told Frankie she was too late, and the Rider and Balkind would have to wait for their breakfast. She smiled again at the memory of the Rider, sitting on the shack's second hand sofa bed and wincing as she dabbed TCP antiseptic onto his cuts. He'd enjoyed the sweet milky tea though, sipping as though he wanted it to last forever, a look of bliss on his face, and both he and Balkind had fallen on the makeshift supper. Beneath her hand, the yale latch turned, snapping her back to the present. Frankie swung the front door open, chanting: 'Come in, come in, you must be soaked …' the words choked in her throat. Instead of her mum and Bally, a menacing figure dressed in black pushed the door open wider, and barged into the hallway, followed by a smaller figure, also dressed in black. It was the police. They had come for her. Frankie clung onto the front door for support, and cursed herself for not looking through the spyhole first.

Without any introductions, the male copper snapped 'Are you Francesca Shaunessy?'

The female officer just stared, her eyes squinting with suspicion under her mono-brow. Frankie hesitated, feeling confirming her name would be like admitting to a crime.

'I'll ask you again, it's a simple question – yes or no – are you Francesca Shaunessy?' The woman pointed her chin aggressively at Frankie as she spoke.

'Yes she is.' Frankie's mum entered the hallway, deftly closing the kitchen door against Bally's nose; she must have come in by the side gate.

'And as you know my daughter's name, you must also know she's a minor. Since you're already in *my* house, we'll go into the front room shall we? And conduct ourselves in a civilised manner.' This last remark was directed at the female officer, who after glancing at her male companion and finding no help there, suddenly found the hallway floor tiles fascinating.

'Take your boots off first, if you don't mind, I don't want mud trodden through my front room.' Frankie's mum was still wearing her own wellies, but the two coppers obediently crouched, and did as ordered. She winked at Frankie over their bent heads. Out loud she said 'Francesca, show the officers into the front room. I'll be giving Bally his breakfast.'

The male officer straightened, his boots in one hand, casting around for a place to put them that wouldn't land him in more trouble. Frankie grinned, unknowingly, they'd broken her mum's sacred rule: "Thou shalt not bully, nor permit a bully to bully others."

'Shall I?' Taking the boots from him, then collecting the woman's boots, Frankie placed them neatly under the hallway table, and led the way into the front room. Once inside, she drew back the curtains, and settled herself onto the one armchair, nodding towards the sofa for the police to sit down. One of Tony's tips: Always keep your enemies in view, don't allow any of 'em to circle around your back. For once, thought Frankie, one of his useless bits of information came in handy. The male cleared his throat, but didn't attempt to speak. The female officer began taking out her notebook and pen, careful not to look at anyone. Frankie knew why they were here: Someone had grassed her up. Either Pete, or Jason, or maybe she'd been spotted sneaking the Rider and his pet griffin into the garden last night. She smiled, but inside her nerves jitterbugged, and she could only hope her mum would send them packing, and soon.

The male officer stood as mum entered the front room, her bare feet squeaking as she walked across the vinyl wooden floor. It seemed she'd sprung out of bed this morning and grabbed the nearest clothes to hand. Tony's dark blue tracksuit swamped her, making her appear waif-like.

'Please Mrs Shaunessy, take a seat.'

Frankie smiled again, then smiled even broader when her mum snapped. 'My name isn't Shaunessy, and that's the first time I've ever been invited to sit in my own home.' She perched on the arm of Frankie's chair. 'Now if you don't mind, my husband is on night duty, so if you'd like to explain why you're here, but quietly.' She flourished her own notebook in one hand, with a pen poised in the other.

'There's no need to be so hostile.' The woman police officer muttered. Frankie's mum stared at her for a semi-beat. 'I agree entirely, perhaps you'll remember that before barging into houses and attempting to question minors without their parents.'

Frankie hugged herself with delight. Then the male officer spoke and her nerves jangled again. 'We've reason to believe your daughter was involved in a serious incident that took place over the village common last night.'

Mum twisted to look at Frankie. 'Is this true – were you over the common last night?'

Frankie dropped her head so she wouldn't have to see the triumph on the woman PC's face.

'Yes mum, I'm sorry mum, I went over to look for Bally's collar.'

'Now that we've established your daughter's been lying to you, we'd like to search the premises.' The woman PC's mono eyebrow twitched with excitement.

'We'd like to start with that outbuilding in the garden.' The male PC added, rising to his feet.

'Oh no you don't!' Frankie's mum shot to her feet too. 'In the first place, Frankie didn't lie to me – she went out to visit a friend, and took a short cut over the common. Is that right Frankie?'

Startled, Frankie nodded her head yes, knowing she'd made a mistake by the flash of satisfaction on both coppers' faces – they had her whereabouts confirmed now.

'Ma'am, we've reason to believe that your daughter's harbouring a man who committed a serious assault on a child last night on Black-Jack's common. We've reasonable grounds to search these premises, with or without your permission – now I'm putting my boots back on – and I'm starting my search with that garden outbuilding.'

Frankie's blood thundered in her ears as her heart raced – she didn't care if she got arrested, but couldn't bear the thought of what might happen to the Rider and Balkind. Michael's voice spoke in her mind: "The best form of defence is attack."

'Assault on a child? Are you talking about Pete Roberts?!' Frankie shouted in disbelief.

'So you *did* witness the assault?' The WPC scribbled something in her notebook.

Trembling, Frankie stuck her arms between her knees, and twisted her hands together, lowering her head again. *Keep quiet fool – keep quiet!* She bit her lip in an effort not to cry.

Mum perched back on the arm of Frankie's chair, and put an arm around her.
'Sit down again the pair of you! If you thought for one second there was a dangerous criminal on these premises, neither of you would have taken your boots off at the front door. We all know that. You're on a fishing trip.'
Frankie breathed a little easier, and the thought occurred to her that if these two plods had played their cards differently, and appealed to mum's better nature, the Rider and Balkind would have been discovered by now. Her mum was married to a copper after all.
'I'll ask you again to keep the noise down – you really don't want to wake my husband.' This second warning came too late. The lounge door creaked open, and Tony lumbered into the lounge. His blood shot eyes swept the room, and the male PC blanched. 'Morning Sarge.' He nudged the WPC, but she appeared to have lost her voice, and merely gaped up at Tony. His short dark hair stood on end, and his white vest puckered slightly over a pot belly, and baggy black track bottoms, but his sergeant stripes could have been tattooed on his biceps.
'PC Blake, WPC ... sorry – I've forgotten your name.'
Her companion nudged her again and the WPC blurted 'Greenbaum sir, I'm WPC Greenbaum.'
Tony nodded, and mooching over to the end of the sofa sunk into the remaining square of seat, next to WPC Greenbaum.
Rubbing at the stubble on his chin, he yawned widely, showing perfect teeth, and uttered his usual greeting to his step-daughter: 'Frankie love, nip and put the kettle on – make the old chap a cuppa.'
Before he'd finished speaking, Frankie flew from the chair and into the kitchen. Bally jumped up to greet her, but she was already at the sink, filling the kettle and splashing water down her front in the process. Frankie slammed the kettle into place, and jabbed the switch on, grabbing a handful of dog biscuits at the same time. Tossing the biscuits in Bally's direction, she scurried out the back door and into the garden in bare feet, heading for the wonky shelter Michael and his mates had cobbled together three years ago to use as a club house. She slapped a warning against the over wide door, really only a piece of ply-board on hinges which served as an entrance, and pushed up the stable latch. Swinging the door open, Frankie puffed out with relief. Apart from a giant spider leering at her from one corner, and a troop of earwigs scuttling away, the place was empty. Once upon a time, Michael and his friends had camped out here. Now all that remained of that long hot summer was a home made display unit hanging on the wall, together with a couple of maps of the British Isles – one showing where fossils were likely to be found, the other showing the best places to locate different types of semi-precious stones. A dark rectangle on the wall hinted that there should be a third map, or poster, would anyone notice?
A hand fell on her shoulder, Frankie gasped out loud and flinched.
'What are you doing out here love?'

Turning, Frankie saw Tony, even worse; PC Blake stood beside him, squinting into the shack.

Frankie nodded towards the young copper, then pointed towards the display unit, trying to sound anxious. 'They worried me – I thought maybe someone had got in here and stolen Michael's collection of stones.'

Tony patted her shoulder, glancing at the younger man he explained 'Frankie's brother's is really into geology.' Tightening his arm around Frankie, he said – 'There – all safe – nothing to worry about.' PC Blake stepped into the shack. Tony stiffened with annoyance. 'You can see for yourself, it's empty. I'd rather you didn't touch anything in here.'

'But there *is* something missing.' PC Blake ignored Tony's warning, and he touched the empty space in the middle of Michael's rock display. Frankie actually felt Tony's hackles rise.

'It isn't missing. I know exactly where the centre piece is, it happens to be on a shelf, in my son's room. Now please come out, else you're going to really pi... pee me off– and you don't want to do that.' Tony had a way of jamming his lips together after each sentence when he was really annoyed.

PC Blake blanched again, and Frankie wondered if he knew that Michael's room was miles from here, in an Essex nursing home. 'Yes sir, I mean no sir.' Gulping visibly he added: 'I'm sorry sir, but I'd still like to ask your daughter some questions.' Tony didn't correct him with "Stepdaughter". Frankie had been given the chance to change her surname to Tony's when mum married him. Out of loyalty, both she and Michael had kept their dad's surname.

'You come back inside and tell us what happened last night.' Tony growled at the copper. 'If Frankie's got anything to add, I'm sure she'll speak up. My daughter has nothing to hide.' Tony said firmly, and more than ever, Frankie wished she *had* changed surnames when given the chance. More than anything, she wished she could confide in mum and Tony, but they had enough to cope with. In any case, the Rider and his griffin were gone now, and no longer her concern.

Chapter ten.

The following day; Sunday, as a kind of unspoken "Thank you" to Tony, Frankie volunteered to accompany mum on her weekly pilgrimage to Essex.

The train halted just outside of Theydon Bois, the next-to-last stop on their two-hour Underground odyssey. Behind her sunglasses, Frankie pretended to doze. She hated riding on the Underground, and she was already dreading the journey home. On the seat next to her, mum clutched her handbag on her lap and sucked a boiled sweet. The convex glass opposite distorted their reflections like a fair ground mirror, turning them into freaks. Disturbed by this image, Frankie looked away. When she did, she saw that they were the only passengers left in this carriage. Her mum hadn't spoken a word for the last eighteen stops. Since Frankie was supposed to be keeping mum company, she thought she should at least try to make conversation.

'We look like two-headed monsters,' she said, pointing at the window.

Mum didn't respond, not even to tell her not to be so childish, and a sudden dread struck Frankie: She was alone on this carriage, and only mum's ghostly reflection remained. Frankie twisted to look at her mum. Silent tears ran down her face.

'Mum, what is it? What's wrong?'

She stared straight ahead and didn't answer. Frankie worried at her mum's fingers, trying to prise them loose from her oversized bag, the "Betty Boop" one Michael had brought back from a school trip to Paris. Her fingers were puffy and, Frankie noticed for the first time, ringless.

'Mum, let me see if you've got a tissue in there, mum, please what's wrong?'

Everything about this journey was wrong of course – they should be going to watch Mikey playing in a football match – not to sit by the side of his cot-bed, and pretend to converse with an animated corpse. But Frankie had never seen her mum crying, not even when Family Liaison at Charring Cross Hospital had first explained to them that Michael was being transferred to a nursing home. 'There's nothing more we can do for your son here,' they had said...

Frankie kept trying to dig into her mum's bag, her mum continued to act as though Frankie wasn't there. Finally she snapped out of her misery. She patted Frankie's hand, and then swiping at her eyes, she took a couple of deep breaths as though making a conscious effort to stop crying.

'It's silly, I'm being silly, don't mind me, go back to sleep – I'll wake you up when we get there.'

Frankie put an arm round her mum's shoulders, a little awkwardly because of the rigid plastic armrest between the two seats.

'Please mum, tell me.'

Her mum's jaw moved again, and she swallowed the sweetie. 'I was just sucking on this fruit drop, and it was so tangy, and making my mouth water, and thinking about what we'll have for dinner tonight.'

'Don't worry about dinner – we'll get take-away.'

'It isn't that – I'm sitting here sucking fruit drops and wondering if we should have lamb or beef for our roast – and Michael – Michael's lying in that – that place – and he's never going to have anything nice to eat again. He's never going to bite into a chocolate cake oozing cream, he's never going to twirl spaghetti round his fork again, and he's never going to even suck on a sweetie.'

Frankie tried to swallow, but an iron rod had somehow wedged in her throat. With an effort, she spoke around the blockage, but her voice came out crackly.

'Oh mum, mum, please don't. Don't give up. You're the one who keeps saying he's going to get better – if it wasn't for you – ' All her mum's wages went on private physiotherapy for Michael. If it wasn't for mum, Michael's limbs would have withered and curled back on themselves long ago.

Her mum's head slumped lower, and Frankie saw a smattering of grey hairs. Before Michael's accident, mum had a standing monthly appointment at the hairdressers, paying extra to have a special dye between red and purple made up for her sleek bob. Now the roots were showing. With a last sigh, she sat upright, and wiped her face with the back of her hand like a child. She shook her head.

'He's already in another world, and only his body's left behind. Maybe it's cruel to keep him here, maybe he's going through torment, and can't tell us. But I can't bear the thought.' She gave an involuntary gasp. 'I can't bear the thought of giving permission then standing by to watch him die.'

The tube train started up with a jerk, inched forward, and then picked up speed. Frankie patted her mum's shoulder.

'That won't happen mum. We'll find a way to reach him, we'll bring him home.'

Her mum didn't reply. The next voice they heard was the nasal drone of the tannoy, five minutes later:

"Epping. This train terminates here. All change."

'Mum, please, you're scaring me.' Frankie said in a small voice. 'We'll bring him home one day, won't we?'

Her mum's lower jaw jutted out, her eyes were a little watery still, but a determined look returned. 'Of course we will. Come on love, let's get going.'

The train may have terminated, but their journey hadn't. They still had a bus ride to take to Romney Marshes, on the East Coast. It occurred to Frankie that Michael's journey hadn't terminated either – and they might be on the losing team, but until the final whistle blew, mum would remain on the sidelines cheering.

They got to their feet, giggling a little at their unsteadiness after the long tube journey. When they started up the stairs leading to the exit and the waiting green-line bus, Frankie tucked her arm through mum's, and she squeezed it against her side as they climbed the stairs together.

Afterwards, on the way home, mum came down with a dose of verbal incontinence. She barely drew breath as she babbled on about this and that: school, work, redecorating the lounge – Frankie guessed her mum would rather think about anything rather than the room they'd spent the last two hours in. Despite the stuffed toy dog, the rugby posters, and even the pot plant, it was sterile, only one step removed from an undertaker's parlour. If Michael's spirit was in another world, Frankie thought, it had better return soon, before his body grew tired of waiting.

Chapter eleven.

On Monday morning, Frankie got to the bus-stop ten minutes early, determined that today nothing would go wrong. Dressed in an immaculate uniform, with her hair neatly braided into one long pigtail, and her shirt starched to a military crispness, she'd left nothing to chance. Even Mr Sharky would smile as she handed in the maths homework...

The maths homework! She'd left it on her desk – in her bedroom! Frankie's stomach did a double flip at the realization. She raced home, fumbling in her bag for her keys as she ran. *Please please please, let the bus be late today!*

She dashed up the driveway to the front door, jabbed the key into the lock, and hurried inside. Bally jumped on her and Frankie pushed him aside, but too late to stop him dribbling over her shirt.

'Down Bally! Kitchen!' She ordered, and he slunk off. She swung around the banister post and, taking the stairs two at a time, charged into her bedroom, snatched up the homework, and glanced at the alarm clock. Eight-forty. Barely enough time to run back to the bus stop, much less change her shirt. She'd have to keep her blazer buttoned and hope for the best.

Frankie ran outside and had made it almost to the garden gate when she *had* to go back, to make certain she'd closed the front door properly. Her mum would go spare if Bally got loose again. 'Oh my God! I'm going to be so late!' She muttered under her breath.

She grabbed the door handle and rattled it. The door was secure. Precious seconds lost, and for nothing. Frankie turned and ran back down the street again, heading for the main road. Twenty yards from the street corner, she spotted the red dome of a bus looming towards the stop.

"Made it!" She puffed, slowing down a little, searching her blazer pocket for her bus pass, and tagging onto a queue of younger school-kids.

The pass wasn't there. She began searching more frantically, jamming her fingers into one pocket after another as the last of the twelve-year-olds bounded onto the bus. The driver stared blankly at Frankie, waiting for her to board.

'I can't find my bus pass!' She told him. He shrugged, and seconds later, the doors closed with a hiss and the bus pulled away, leaving Frankie standing there. Two faces appeared in the bus's rear window, Year 8 kids whom she knew by sight. They smirked and grimaced at her, and threw in a couple of rude gestures for good measure. Blinking away tears of frustration, Frankie slouched against the bus shelter's frame, wishing she could go home and back to bed, when suddenly she saw a silver car approaching, sunlight dancing from its roof.

Tony! On his way home from taking mum to work! The answer to all her prayers!

Straightening up, Frankie waved, standing on tip-toe so he'd be sure to notice her. Tony waved back, smiling happily, and drove straight past – on his way to the golf course for an early morning round of golf with a fellow night shift worker.

Frankie should have realised the universe didn't want her to go to school that day, but she started walking there anyway. It was over a mile away. At least now, she thought, things can't get any worse.

When Frankie walked into the school-office, the clock on the wall showed nine twenty-seven. She signed the "late register" under a battery of glares from the school secretaries, and headed for the English block. Handing in the maths homework would have to wait until break-time: She was twenty minutes late, and she didn't dare interrupt Mr Sharky's lesson.

Frankie hesitated outside of English Room Four. Without the sound of her footsteps echoing along the empty corridor, a silence descended, and her nervousness increased. She couldn't hear any noise, not even the rustling of paper. Easing the door open Frankie peered into the room, seeking Annette's mass of curly brown hair, and preparing to scuttle into the empty desk next to her. Instead she saw Chardonnay Lombard sitting next to her best friend, with a look of smugness on her piggy face. Annette didn't look around.

'Can I help you?'

Frankie almost jumped back into the corridor. Instead of their usual English teacher, a washed-out hippy who made everyone call him Charlie, a woman stood in front of the teacher's desk. At first glance, she didn't seem any older than the class, but that couldn't be right. She must be at least twenty. So a student teacher then – but one with enough authority to keep a group of Year 11's in line.

'Come in or go out – but make up your mind.' The woman said, her arched eyebrow almost reaching to her fringe, which swept over her brow to join the rest of her sleek dark mane. Even wearing blue jeans and a paler blue short sleeved shirt, she had an air of elegance about her that made Frankie feel untidy, especially with her blazer buttoned tightly around her waist, and her shirt clinging to her skin. Glancing around the room, looking for an empty desk, Frankie noticed something strange: apart from Chardonnay's gloat, everyone else was continuing to study as though their lives depended on reading the textbook in front of them. Usually a late-comer's arrival caused heads to swivel and even the odd cat-call.

Frankie spotted an empty desk behind Chelsi and Poppy, and made her way down the centre aisle towards it; keeping her head down and mumbling; 'sorry I'm late – I missed the bus.'

Frowning, the young woman swivelled to stretch for the class register on the far side of the desk behind her. Frankie slid into the empty seat. After consulting the register for a few seconds the teacher looked up at Frankie and said:

'I don't suppose you're Peter Roberts, so you must be Francesca Shaunessy. Am I right?'

'Yes miss,' Frankie mumbled, searching through her school bag for her English books.

'Look at me when you're speaking to me please, and don't mumble.' She stalked over to Frankie's desk as she spoke, holding a text book. It landed with a thwack on the desk. A manicured nail tapped the cover, and the heavy gold bangles around the teacher's wrist jangled.

'Turn to page thirty – and try to keep up.' Swivelling on her heel, she stalked back to her desk and turned to address the class. 'Okay, another ten minutes, then I want you to choose any character in this chapter, and describe his or her personality.'

Frankie opened the book—*Romeo and Juliet*— and shuddered. Over the next forty minutes, she learned three things: Firstly their new teacher's name was Miss Gerraty, secondly, Peter Roberts wouldn't be coming back to school this term, and thirdly, there was a rumour sweeping the school that Frankie was a witch. Ford Henderson dropped the last two bombshells in the form of a scribbled note, when Miss Gerraty told him to open a window.

Frankie spent the whole lesson staring at the same words on the same page. From time to time Miss Gerraty's sharp voice cut into the class's silence, as she read aloud her favourite quotations. It seemed she didn't require any response, and after she finished speaking, the returning silence was even more oppressive.

At long last the bell rang. Heads rose expectantly, but everyone remained in their seats. Miss Gerraty surveyed the class with smugness of a cat, pleased with their mouse-like meekness.

'Make sure your name is at the top of your work.' She pointed to the row of desks against the far wall. 'This aisle, papers on my desk and text books on another pile, and leave my classroom quietly.' It's impossible for twelve teenagers to leave a room quietly, in the subdued hub-bub that followed, Chelsi and Poppy swung round to Frankie, wide eyed.

'What happened on Friday night?' Chelsi whispered. But Miss Gerraty heard her. 'I did NOT give permission to talk. You'll be in the playground in two minutes, until then, turn around and be quiet.'

Chelsi flushed, but she turned around. After raising her eyebrows at Frankie, Poppy turned to face the front too. The first row to be dismissed left the classroom. Having made certain everything was to her liking again, Miss Gerraty dismissed the next aisle, which was Frankie's row. Chelsi and Poppy were talking to her, but Annette wasn't, her mind worried at this, as she scraped her chair back.

'Not you, Francesca Shaunessy. Remain in your seat, please.'

Chelsi managed a quick grimace at Frankie before flitting out into the corridor. *I really should have stayed in bed today,* Frankie told herself again. Finally, the very last student walked out the door and pulled it closed behind him.

Frankie kept her arms folded on the desk, her back straight, and her eyes downcast. Miss Gerraty perched on Chelsi's desk, and folded her arms too.

'Don't ignore me, Francesca. You've got a serious attitude problem, and I want to know why.'

Frankie glanced up, Miss Gerraty's eyes rested on her with concern, but still managed to convey a sharpness. Something told Frankie that the teacher could see right through her, and would be quick to punish any BS.

Frankie nearly blurted everything out – how her life had turned upside down for the second time in three years, because she'd accidentally summoned a griffin from another dimension. But thankfully Miss Gerraty started talking first.

'You come into my lesson half an hour late; glaring around the class – distracting Chelsi and Poppy – and I saw Henderson passing you notes.' Frankie blinked – how – did she have eyes in the back of her head?

'But ...but,' Frankie stammered.

'As if that wasn't bad enough,' Miss Gerraty continued, 'you actually shuddered when I gave the class an assignment – and you haven't written a word! It's nothing to smile about!'

But Frankie couldn't help grinning. Despite appearing all-knowing, she was the same as all the other adults. Jumping to conclusions.

'I'm really sorry Miss Gerraty, I'll try harder I promise. Can I go now? I've got to hand some homework into the staff room.'

'You may leave, once you've explained why you find the works of Shakespeare so repulsive.'

Wrong again, Francesca. Frankie told herself, and frowned. 'I don't. I just don't like *Romeo and Juliet*. I think it's silly.'

Miss Gerraty straightened, pushing herself up from the desk.

'Silly? A play that's enthralled the world for centuries, and you find it silly?'

'Not silly, that's the wrong word. Unnecessary – if Romeo had told his parents to back off, and Juliet had stood up for herself, then the whole—'

'—tragedy would never have happened.' Miss Gerraty finished for her, and to Frankie's astonishment, she smiled. 'Do you have any romance in your soul?'

Frankie shrugged, and feeling the back of her neck burning, tugged at her shirt collar.

'Shakespeare wrote his play to be unforgettable,' Miss Gerraty continued. If everything worked out happily ever after in the end, Romeo and Juliet wouldn't—'

'They wouldn't have died!' Frankie shouted. 'They would have grown old together and they wouldn't have died!'

Frankie's outburst surprised her as much as it did Miss Gerraty. The teacher recovered first. Licking one finger, and smoothing back a tendril of hair, she said coldly 'Well people do die – even young people – even in real life.'

'Really?' Frankie stooped to collect her bag, blinking back tears. 'I've got to go – else I'll be late handing in my homework,' she was already late with it 'and late for my next lesson.'

She'd almost made it to the door when Miss Gerraty called out. 'Not so fast. You've just earned yourself detention for tonight.'

Teachers could hand out same day half an hour's detention without notice. Anything longer and parents had to be informed. Frankie paused just long enough to say, 'sorry miss, I've already got detention. Some other time – eh?' With that she stormed down the corridor, heading for the opposite end of the school, preparing for her next ordeal.

Maisy Shearing and her friend, *(Maxine? Lucy?* Frankie couldn't quite place the pallid little face), were propped against a radiator outside the senior girls' toilets. Maisy nudged the other girl as Frankie walked past, and she heard muttering behind her back.

Frankie bristled, she usually went out of her way to say 'Hi' to Maisy. The thirteen-year-old still wore glasses with a white eye-patch over the left lens to correct a squint, so most kids saw her as an easy target to tease. Frankie turned to glare, surprised when both Maisy and her friend shrunk back against the radiator, clinging to it with white knuckled fingers. Maisy's good eye appeared enormous, while her face turned the colour of her eye-patch.

'What's wrong Maisy?' Although asked in a gentle tone, some of her irritation must have leaked out. Without answering, the two misfits scurried away, prepared to brave the playground bullies rather than talk to Frankie.

Frowning, she dismissed the silly little kids, and a few seconds later, she rapped loudly on the staff room door. It opened immediately, Mr Sharky must have been waiting behind it to pounce on her.

'Ah, Miss Shaunessy – at last! I see you finally found the staff room.'

Really? He'd had all morning to think up sarcastic remarks and that was the best he could come up with? Smiling politely, Frankie handed in her homework. His cheeks worked as his eyes scanned the neatly written answers, checked and double checked.

'Excellent, excellent. It seems basic algebra's too simple for you. Tonight, we'll try more complicated problems.' It was his turn to smile. 'If two hours' detention isn't long enough for you to grasp the theory, I'll make certain there's plenty of homework for you to practise with.' Somehow Frankie managed to keep smiling, at least until she turned to walk away.

Sharky's sarcasm was nothing compared to what waited for her in the playground: Frankie really should have taken a hint from the universe, and stayed in bed that day.

Chapter twelve.

Frankie barged out of the glass fire exit door into the smaller playground reserved for the seniors in Year Ten and Eleven. As usual, the popular girls had called shot-gun on the best bench; Chelsi and Poppy, together with Emily Tomlinson and Summer Wilson held court. As usual, a boy perched either side of Chelsi and her girls, balancing on the wide wooden arm rests. In front of the bench, a group of boys knocked a football around, trying to impress, even though Chelsi and her set were way out of their league. Chelsi sat with her shoulders hunched, and her hands in her blazer pockets, tugging the maroon material tightly around herself, as though she were cold.

Frankie decided she wouldn't be miserable if she had half the attention Chelsi got, and wondered again how she did it. Then she thought that if you have to ask what makes the cool kids cool, you were never gonna *be* cool in a million zillion years.

Frankie marched diagonally towards the collection of benches and picnic tables located at the other end of the playground, under a group of trees, hoping to find Annette there. The senior playground was never as noisy as the junior playground, but today it seemed strangely silent. Frankie skirted groups of students, puzzled when Linda Reade and Perminda Patel, both of whom she'd known forever, didn't say 'Hi' or return her smiles. By now, even the smack of a ball bouncing against asphalt had stopped. Frankie's pace slowed, and she looked around, searching for a reason for this unnatural hush. Perhaps the school's principal had entered the playground ... with a rush of embarrassment, she realised every single student's attention was directed at her. Her face burned, and she sweltered more than ever under her blazer. She wanted to retreat, to get out of here, but like some crumbly zombie movie, students began shuffling their way towards Frankie. They muttered to each other as they approached; their eyes met Frankie's but only for an instant, before skittering away again. Frankie searched for a friendly face, and spotted Joy Lewis and Karen McGregor. 'Hi Joy, hi Karen, what's up?' She asked breezily.

Joy's long upper lip pulled back from her teeth, and Karen seemed confused that Frankie had spoken, as though she had no right to address either of them. They faltered, the crowd surged, and Simon Bishop's permanently red face hovered inches from Frankie's.

'Witch!' He spat.

Frankie recoiled, wiping spittle from her cheek with a grimace of distaste. 'What?!'

'Witch!' A second voice called, as Simon repeated the word, and before Frankie could respond, it seemed the whole playground surrounded her, chanting 'Witch! Witch! Witch!'

Ford Henderson barged through the sea of maroon blazers towards Frankie, shoving Simon aside. Simon spun, his fist flew out and punched Ford's temple, sending him sprawling against Joy Lewis. Frankie stooped to help him up, and someone snatched her school bag from her shoulder. Seconds later Frankie's packed lunch, so carefully prepared by her mum last night, came flying towards her. A cellophane covered sandwich hit above Frankie's right eye, a sachet of orange juice exploded against her head, and all the time the spiteful chant of 'Witch' filled her ears. Clinging onto Ford somewhere around his waist, Frankie ducked her head, trying to burrow away from the mob surrounding her, terrified of what they would do next.

'Stop it! Stop this!' Somehow Chelsi was at Frankie's other side, her eyes blazing as she shouted down the chanting. 'Poppy's getting Miss Prater, and I'm telling that you, you and you,' Chelsi pointed accusingly into the crowd as she spoke 'were throwing stuff at Frankie. You're all in trouble anyway.'

'Why are you sticking up for her? She almost killed her own brother, and nearly murdered your boyfriend!' Joy rattled the words out. 'Yeah – why do you wanna stick up for a witch?' Simon yelled the last word, as though hoping the chant would be taken up again.

'I didn't nearly kill anyone – so shut your mouth Joy Lewis!' Frankie shouted, suddenly furious. 'Thanks Chelsi, but I can look after myself.' Letting go of Ford, she straightened her skirt, and pushed sticky strands of hair from her forehead.

Puffing out with exasperation, Chelsi snatched Frankie's bag back from a shamed face looking Karen. Chelsi's arm snaked around Frankie's waist, and placing her hand square on Simon's face, she pushed him out the way and marched Frankie from the playground and into school. They met Miss Prater, the school principal, clacking along in the corridor, with Poppy scurrying behind her. 'Chelsi, Francesca, what's going on?'

Chelsi nodded towards the playground. 'Ford Henderson and Simon Bishop are fighting. Simon Bishop started it.' Glancing through the half glazed corridor, Frankie saw Chelsi was right. Simon might have started the fight, but it seemed Ford was going to finish it. A "look" passed between Chelsi and Poppy, who nodded her head, and then smiled at Frankie, before hurrying to catch Miss Prater up again.

Chelsi shouldered open the swing door of the senior girls' toilets, and hustled Frankie inside. A free standing partition lined with mirrors, with wash-hand basins underneath ran through the middle of the room, with four cubicles either side. Bizarrely, on the end wall, for some reason there was a wide shelf, and above this, grey metal coat hooks, jutting from the wall at regular intervals. Whether the designer thought the "senior girls" might enjoy strip down washes at the hand basins was anybody's guess, but the shelf made a convenient make-shift seat. Chelsi steered Frankie over there now, and propped her up on the shelf. Then Chelsi hitched herself up, she started to speak, but the door creaked open and a girl in the year below them entered. Casting a shy glance at the older girls, she scuttled into one of the cubicles.

The door creaked open again, and Poppy entered, grinning cheerfully. Frankie remembered that she hadn't spoken properly to either of her classmates since Michael's accident, and why. Scowling, she wriggled down from the shelf. Poppy darted over and pressed her back onto the makeshift seat. 'Stay there – we want a word with you.'

Frankie pushed her away, but then Chelsi started on her.

'Shuddup and listen. And don't glare at me like that.'

'Oh for heaven's sake! What is this? I'm not some charity case – don't pretend we were ever friends or anything.'

'We *were* friends; we've never stopped being friends. It's you – you're like a porcupine and won't let anyone near you. I'm sorry - we're all sorry about Michael.'

Frankie stared at Chelsi; her big soulful eyes flickered away for a moment, then stared steadily back.

'I know you blame me.'

'Too right!'

'But don't you see – it wasn't just me putting Michael off balance – be fair Frankie – he only clipped his skull against that headstone, and when we *did* call for an ambulance – the driver went to the wrong St Mary's ...'

'The catholic church.' Poppy interjected

'And the vicar had locked the gates – to keep out the doggers and lampers.'

'If you want to blame anyone, you might as well blame the headstone – it was just a series of events waiting to happen – like – I dunno –'

'The Titanic.' The Year 10 girl earwigging in as she washed her hands supplied helpfully. All three girls glared at the younger girl. Mumbling a 'sorry' she slunk away without drying her hands.

'You can't do this to yourself Frankie – It's like you're punishing yourself because Michael's ...' Chelsi's voice trailed off, as Frankie glared at her, daring her to say it.

'Do you think Michael would want this – you shutting out your friends, never talking to anyone, apart from that swot Annette?' Poppy said, a tone of impatience creeping into her voice.

'You know nothing about my brother – '

Tossing her head and swirling her hair back like a model in a corny shampoo advert, Poppy slid from the shelf in one graceful movement.

'Come on Chelsi, didn't I tell you we were wasting our time? I'm going – come on or we'll be late for our next lesson.'

'Wait up Poppy, I'm coming with you.' Chelsi leaned back, preparing to swing down from the shelf, and clunked her head against a coat hook. 'Ouch!' She said, and catching Frankie's eye, dissolved into giggles. After a second or two, Frankie joined in. She'd completely forgotten this side of Chelsi, how she was always ready to laugh, even at herself. Frankie felt a twinge of guilt, in her heart, she knew she'd been punishing not only herself, but her friends. She wasn't ready to apologise, not yet, but she tried to mend fences.

'Thanks for helping me – in the playground I mean.' Frankie blurted.

'Simon Bishop's such a twat – everyone knows witches have red hair and green eyes!' Chelsi seemed eager to steer the conversation away from Michael too. 'Do you want to borrow ...' She indicated her own glossy hair 'You've got food in your hair.' She fussed around in her bag, and producing a hairbrush, handed it to Frankie. 'Thanks Chelsi.' Loosening her hair from its pigtail, Frankie began brushing out the stickiness.

'Your hair's a lovely colour, so thick too.' Chelsi told her. Frankie grimaced: Nearly everyone made that comment – as though they were trying to persuade her that it wasn't so bad being a red head.

'No, really – think of all the great gingers – Boudica, Elizabeth the First ...' running out of names Chelsi added lamely 'Karen Gillan – honest – you're so lucky.'

The door eased open, and Ford's head appeared around the side. 'Ford, don't you think Frankie's got lovely hair?' Chelsi called, sounding relieved to have back up. Ford's face softened, as he surveyed both girls, and he nodded agreement. 'Frankie's got lovely everything,' he said cheerfully, adding 'you okay Frankie?' and pushing the door fully open, he entered the girls' loos. Frankie noticed that he did glance at the cubicles, to check they were all alone, but still, she thought, if he was caught in here, he'd probably be suspended from school or something. 'Thanks for sticking up for me,' she muttered, bundling her hair back into a scrunchie again. Ford swung himself up beside Frankie, patted her knee awkwardly and said 'anytime.' Bemused, Frankie looked away, then up at Chelsi. She was staring at Ford as though seeing him for the first time, and Frankie squirmed unhappily. Although Frankie barely admitted it even to herself, she'd had a crush on Ford since Year 9. His dark brown hair curled slightly away from a broad forehead, and he had dreamy brown eyes and a square-ish chin, with a small cleft to it. It kinda drew attention to his full lips, smiling at her now, and Frankie felt a sudden flush of pleasure. A good looking boy preferred her to Chelsi, how could that be? Frankie wriggled uncomfortably, then jumped down. 'We'd better get back to lessons,' she muttered. Ford jumped down too, standing inches from Frankie. She caught a whiff of tea tree and fresh mint, and knew suddenly he used the same shower gel as she did, and that imagery made her blush.

'I'll walk you to your class.' Ford said, snatching her bag from the shelf. 'See you Chelsi.'

Slinging Frankie's bag over one shoulder, and his other arm across Frankie's shoulders, he walked her over to the door. Frankie twisted her head around to peer back at Chelsi, who grinned at Frankie's obvious bewilderment, jabbing both thumbs up. Still amazed at this sudden change in fortune, Frankie let Ford do all the talking as he accompanied her along the corridor, up one flight of stairs, then along another corridor to Frankie's history class.

'I should be at work experience right now,' Ford said as they paused outside the classroom door. 'But I'll come back to school afterwards, and walk you home – okay?' Before Frankie could say yes or no, he shrugged her bag from his shoulder, and hurried back down the corridor, and then turned to clatter down the stairs and out of sight.

For the second time that morning, Frankie was late for class. This time though, she entered the room as though she owned it. History was one of Frankie's favourite subjects, and Mr Walters one of her favourite teachers. After glaring at Simon Bishop, who wouldn't meet her eyes, Frankie apologised for being late. Mr Walters didn't ask for an excuse, maybe the school grapevine had been buzzing. Ignoring the empty seat next to Annette, Frankie marched along the desk aisles, and slid into the "Teacher's Pet" seat at the front.

Strange really, she mused, she'd gone from wondering what made cool kids cool to being cool herself. All it took was a little confidence: From now on, she decided, everything was going to be different and her life was going to be extra-ordinarily normal.

<<<<<*****>>>>>

When the last bell went, Frankie walked through the school gates, and caught a glimpse of Ford's dark tousled hair as he headed a football, playing keepsie up with a group of kids from Year 7 and 8. Spotting Frankie, Ford carelessly toed the football to one of the youngsters and hurried over to her side. He wore track suit bottoms over a sleeveless vest. The grey cotton material fitted his chest snugly, hinting at well defined muscles, and emphasising his broad shoulders. Everyone knew three football scouts had already approached him, not that Ford boasted, there'd been an article in the local newspaper. Feeling envious eyes on her, Frankie felt another rush of pleasure, as Ford took her school bag from her, and fell into step beside her. After an initial "Hi", they walked in silence across the village green, past the post-office, the mini-supermarket, and a collection of wanna-be antique shops. An old "Star-Wars" poster was yellowing in one of the junk-shop's windows. Searching for some conversation Frankie said 'is that who you're named after – Harrison Ford?' A dimple appeared in Ford's cheek, and he flushed as he answered 'I wish.' Glancing left and right to make certain no secondary school students were within earshot he continued 'If I tell you, promise you won't tell anyone else?' He grinned again, showing two dimples this time, and a flash of white teeth. Frankie swallowed, he really was seriously good looking, any moment now he'd realise his mistake in walking *her* home. She traced a cross against her upper blazer pocket and whispered 'promise.'

'My mum and dad went on honeymoon in a place called "Wallingford", I was born nine months later.' He glanced at Frankie, to see if she got the joke. Frankie felt a twinge of pity, before the laughter bubbled out of her. The laughter was partly relief, Ford must *really* like her, to trust her with such an embarrassing secret. Bad enough to think of your crinklies making out, but to be reminded of it every time they called your name ... Grinning widely at her amusement, Ford continued to keep her in fits of giggles as he speculated on other weird and wonderful place names he could have been named after. When Frankie recovered enough, she joined in: 'Brown Willy, Lower Dicker ...' They were walking along Church Road now, only a mile left to go, and it was all downhill to Frankie's house. Just before they turned into Frankie's street, the school bus overtook them, and halted to allow passengers on and off. The same group of kids who'd taken the mickey out of Frankie this morning, now eyed her respectfully, mumbling greetings to Ford, as they scurried past. Out of habit, Frankie began fiddling with her house keys, the aim was to get indoors before Bally could bark and wake Tony up.

Ford's steps slowed. 'So here we are, I've walked you home.' He said, and seemed to be waiting for something. Frankie licked her lips nervously, then wished she hadn't drawn attention to her lips. Should she kiss him? Would he kiss her? Would he expect tongues? Should she put her tongue in his mouth? Would their noses get in the way? Should she close her eyes? To put off the evil moment, Frankie stammered 'would you like to come inside? For a coffee – or something?' *Oh hell, why did I say "or something?" "Come in for a coffee" sounded grown-up, the "or something" sounded odd.* Her cheeks burned, and she knew she was flushing.

'I thought your dad worked nights – will it be okay?' Ford didn't seem to notice her confusion, and Frankie breathed a sigh of relief at his concern for Tony's sleep patterns.

'Don't worry, Tony can sleep through "Call of Duty", so I'm sure he won't wake up.'

Ford's face brightened – 'Wow – you've got "COD"? What level are you on?' By now Frankie had the front door open, and her hand around Bally's muzzle. Ford stepped forward to make a fuss over the mutt, who was wagging his whole body with delight, while Frankie tiptoed into the kitchen to make coffee as quietly as she could.

Half an hour later, Frankie slumped in the armchair, opposite Tony and Ford, who were engrossed in conversation on the sofa, with Bally between them. They enthused about fitness training regimes and the new gym club that had opened in a nearby town, and the coming football season. Apparently, even in his sleep, Tony could tell the difference between Frankie making coffee for her and Annette, and Frankie making coffee for her and Ford. As Frankie placed two coffee cups on a tray, Tony had thundered down the stairs and straight into the lounge. At least he'd bothered to pull on shorts and a tee-shirt. For the hundredth time, Frankie cringed inside, wondering what Ford must be thinking. At that moment, Ford looked over at her, and winked, and then stood up. 'Nice meeting you, Tony; thanks for the coffee, Frankie, I'd better make a move now though.'

Tony stood up too, saying: 'I'll give you a lift home, son.'

When Ford protested 'I'm only at the other end of the village, I can jog back.' Tony smirked and repeated 'I'll give you a lift home,' in a tone that said "no arguments."

Five minutes later, as the rumble of Tony's engine died away, Frankie said to an empty house 'Thanks a lot, Tony!' Ford would never offer to walk her home again, and now she'd never discover how to kiss a boy.

Chapter thirteen.

The Rider tipped his pool lounger back a little and reclined, tilting his face towards the sun's rays. *When my skin dries, I'll get back to work*, he promised himself.

He had barely closed his eyes when footsteps sounded on the mezzanine tiles surrounding the swimming pool. He sprang from the chair and snatched up a robe, hurriedly thrusting his arms into the sleeves and tying the belt around his waist.

'Aha my boy – you've been taking advantage of the late autumn sunshine,' said his host.

The Rider stared. Professor Chown returned the gaze, examining him in the same way a hungry man surveyed a buffet table. The dainty and dapper little man was dressed in his usual three piece suit. Today's pinstripe was red against charcoal grey. The Rider continued to meet the professor's eyes, and even managed to smile. What he had discovered last night only confirmed his growing suspicion: Accepting the professor's invitation might yet prove to be the biggest mistake of his life. Despite appearances, Chown was more dangerous than a flight of dragons.

'I've transcribed two chapters since last night, professor – I gave the tapes to your secretary this morning.' He mentally held his breath.

'No need for excuses, my boy. No need for excuses. After all, you've almost finished.' He moved a wicker garden chair a couple of feet, then sat close to the younger man and squeezed his knee through the towelling robe. The Rider shuddered at the unwanted physical contact.

'I wonder if today, you might allow me to meet with your griffin,' said the professor.

The Rider shook his head.

'I'm sorry, they don't really come out of hibernation until it's sizzling hot. He'll still be grumpy and shedding feathers.' He had given the same response to this same question for the past six days now. Griffins *didn't* hibernate. In fact, he didn't know the term existed until recently. The professor had unwittingly provided the word, in response to the Rider's first stuttering excuses. Of course, that had been before learning of the professor's real intent towards Balkind.

But for now the Rider breathed another silent sigh of relief. Once again the smug little man nodded acceptance. Professor Chown believed himself to be so superior in intellect, it never occurred to him the Rider might be lying.

'Quite so, quite so. It's just that my friends and I are eager to see this magnificent beast.'

The Rider smiled, shuddering inwardly again. He suspected that he owed his liberty, if not his life to the fact that Balkind remained hidden.

At first, Professor Chown had seemed sent by the gods. Down to the last few notes that served in this world as a promise to pay a pound weight in gold, and with nowhere to go, the Rider had discovered buildings called libraries. Here one could sit in warmth and comfort; and while he had yet to work out how the moving images inside the little windows worked, he had discovered picture books. Even better, one of the librarians had gently suggested he try "Talking Books," and he readily accepted her offer to obtain tapes of books on other dimensions, and mythical beasts.

He had been surprised when the author of the book he was listening to made an appearance at the library. Even more so when the learned man fell into conversation with him. Professor Chown knew a lot about other dimensions, something about dragons, and a little about griffins. Swearing him to secrecy, the professor revealed that his mansion in Oxfordshire housed a collection of artefacts belonging to visitors from other worlds.

With his gleaming pink skin and twinkling blue eyes, Professor Chown seemed harmless – even his fingernails were manicured. Since they were sharing secrets, and since the "experts" on other worlds could only offer theories, and he was becoming increasingly desperate, the Rider confessed that he was from another dimension. Then and there in the library, they'd struck a pact: the Rider would help Chown understand more about his collection, and the professor would try to help him find a way home.

Since then, he'd come to realise that the meeting was engineered. Maybe all librarians had orders to report anyone overly interested in other worlds, maybe the books themselves were flagged in some way. A cloud drifted over the sun. The professor gave an exaggerated shiver. Then he slapped the Rider's knee.

'Get dressed,' he told him. 'You'll catch your death of cold.'

Then the professor stood up, tugged at his trouser material to readjust the knife sharp crease, and walked back inside his mansion, humming as he went.

The Rider waited a few minutes before walking over to the patio table. Picking up a sheaf of velum papers, he pulled out a chair and sitting down at the table, settled back to work. He studied the rune like symbols as though composing a translation in his mind before activating the hand-held tape recorder. But that was just in case anyone watched him covertly. The Rider would translate the printed symbols later. For now, his fingers stroked over the velum. There, embossed by tiny bumps which a blind person might consider to be Braille, except Braille written in a foreign language, was the real message left behind by Leifur, a former Lord of Ella-Earth. Laying in his bunk, the Rider often read late into the night. To conserve his meagre ration of candles, he always used the "darkness" method of reading. Lord Leifur's warnings were as clear as day.

"I should not have trusted Professor Chown. Today, the Wessex-Stone disappeared. I know he, or one of his minions have taken it. I begin to fear for my life."

The Rider swallowed down his own unease, and turning on the tape recorder, began to speak. Telling tales of Ella-Earth without actually giving any useful information was one way to while away the hours. The Rider discovered he quite enjoyed inventing stories. Now he launched into an imaginary day in the life of a griffin rider, according to "The Journals of Lord Leifur." When he'd finished, the sun was directly overhead. A homely smell of onions and gravy drifted through the patio doors, along with the faintest tinkle of cutlery. It must be nearing lunchtime, and he still wasn't dressed. With a last glance towards the pool, the Rider stood, and began to gather Leifur's papers together. He froze suddenly, and ran his fingers over the raised dots again. How did he miss this? Why hadn't he continued reading in the darkness manner?

"The fateful hour nears. Chown has discovered Sleipnir. I fear I will never see my son grow into a man." The Rider's mind raced – Sleipnir was the fleetest and bravest of all griffins; named for Odin's legendary mount. But Leifur had no children; no heirs. Every time the remaining three guardians met, they quarrelled horribly over Leifur's estate. Griffin Master Romulus always returned from these meetings in an even fouler mood than usual, but he had to attend; he was Lord Leifur's deputy.

'Professor Chown's waiting for you in the dining room.' A clipped tone interrupted the Rider's musing.

Miss Snodson; beige in face and dress, and housekeeper to Professor Chown stood at his shoulder, trying to peer at the papers he still clutched in his hand.

'Thank you, I'll be five minutes.'

Her lips clenched together, and her sharp chin jutted with disapproval. The Rider knew she referred to him as "That Alien" and hated waiting on him; hated him in fact. Within a few days of his arrival, she'd taken to wearing a belt around her waist. Attached to the belt was a ridiculously small blade, a black handled kitchen knife. Doubtless if she ever got an excuse though, she'd plunge it into his eyes or somewhere equally painful. Of more interest to the Rider was the batch of keys that hung from Miss Snodson's belt. They would unlock every room and door in Chown's mansion. He needed those keys, and he needed them soon – to escape from this place.

<<<<<*****>>>>>

The Rider watched Professor Chown dabbing at his mouth with a napkin. He wondered again how such a frail looking old man could put away so much food and still remain so skeletal.

Catching his eye, Professor Chown said 'My father considered offal to be peasant's food, but I do enjoy eating heart, especially lamb's-heart.'

The Rider ate everything put in front of him, with a soldier's mentality: "Eat while you can, you never know when your next meal will be served." Or what it would be either. Even so, he grimaced internally, while managing to keep a polite expression on his face. But the professor's next words shocked him.

'Fascinating to think that griffins have three hearts.'

How could he possibly know that? The Rider lowered his eyes to his plate quickly. Lord Leifur's journals began in high spirits. He had journeyed here, to this other world, hoping to have peace talks with the Uninvited in their own lands. But right from the start, wily Lord Leifur ensured his griffin was concealed from Professor Chown, and had been guarded in his speech. As desperation crept into his writing, Leifur admitted he had made a mistake, and vowed never to reveal Sleipnir's whereabouts to the professor. So how did Chown know that griffins had two secondary hearts, which were used to pump blood throughout their giant wings?

The door swept open, and Professor Chown's chauffeur entered the room. A few days ago, the Rider would have gladly traded griffin talk for a conversation about cars with Shaf. Now the Rider watched covertly as Shaf bent to whisper to Professor Chown, and wondered idly why he kept his hair covered in a turban. The professor's eyes widened, flinging his napkin to the table, he pushed his chair back and stood up.

The Rider automatically stood up too. Chown marched around the vast dining table, stopping inches from the Rider's face. He peered upwards, with a smug smile. 'We may be making progress.'

Chown's smugness increased, as he sensed the Rider's confusion. Smiling even wider, he reached up to flick an imaginary piece of fluff from the Rider's shoulder.

'I think your griffin is about to come out of hibernation.'

Chapter fourteen.

Towards the end of October, Frankie strolled along a path scattered with jewelled leaves, watching white sails flitting across silvery waters, listening to Bally's joyful bark and moorhens squawking. The kindest sweetest boy in school had his arm around her, as they walked around Trey Lake. A Red Admiral butterfly flopped onto Ford's sleeve. Scooping it from his jumper, Ford coaxed the fragile insect onto Frankie's finger. She allowed it to rest there for a second or two, a ring fit for a princess, and then carefully placed it on the bark of a sycamore tree. She'd been wrong about two things: Ford continued to walk her home every evening after school, and she discovered not only how to kiss boys, but that she quite enjoyed kissing boys, or rather this particular boy, and she did so now. Still holding her tightly, Ford nuzzled his head against her ear, and said 'I'm going to miss you so much.' Frankie sighed, pulling away from his embrace, but keeping a hold of Ford's hand, and they continued walking. The sun shone just above the horizon, and everything its rays touched appeared to be lit from within. This time next week, due to the clocks going back, it would be dark at this hour of day. Frankie wanted to tell Ford her whole world would seem darker without him, but didn't. The invitation to train with City's Under Twenty-Ones was a golden opportunity. This could be the start of his dreams of playing football professionally coming true, and Ford deserved all the support and encouragement she could give.

'Next time you come home, everything will be different. You, me – and Michael – will come out here to watch the sailing boats!' Desperate not to show her sadness, Frankie ducked her head against his chest, listening to his heart beat.

Ford's voice rumbled against her ear, 'You, me and Michael? You forgot Bally!' Hearing his name, the dopey dog bounded over and jumped up at them. Frankie stroked Bally's velvety fur, her fingers tangling with Ford's, and a memory of the other Balkind played in her mind. *I hope he made it back to his own world.* She thought, a little guiltily, before consoling herself that there'd been no further sightings of a random griffin on the loose. For the briefest moment of time, the Rider's image shimmered in front of her, his strange intense eyes appeared to be imploring her, and his words echoed through her mind:

"Call with all your heart, and he will come to you."

Shaking her head to rid herself of the vision, Frankie muttered angrily, 'No he won't. He's in his own world. He *must* be in his own world.'

Ford's arm tightened around her shoulders, and his lips brushed her temple. 'Don't worry little shortie. We'll get him back.'

After a stab of confusion, Frankie realised Ford thought she was talking about Michael, and it seemed easier to nod and smile and agree. A voice shattered the tranquillity by declaring "Yoh! I got the world in my wallet –" Ford glanced down at the mobile in his hand, and mouthing "It's your mum" accepted the call. Frankie groaned, every hour on the hour! Smiling at her, Ford nodded his head against the phone: 'No worries Mrs Fletcher, we're heading back now, I'll have Frankie home soon as.' Frankie scowled at him, but Ford laughed at her protests. 'Your mum sounds really hyped, there's some professor or other, wants to talk about Michael.' He grinned, as he spun her round to walk in the opposite direction, and whistled to Bally. With a squeeze of her shoulders he said 'weird, we were just chatting about Michael being here with us this time next year – maybe this is it Frankie! This guy might be the answer to all our prayers.' Frankie loved him for saying that, but a thought nagged her. The world rarely offered something for nothing, and she wondered what this stranger would ask for in return.

<<<<<*****>>>>>

Chelsi had persuaded Frankie's mum into having something called a "beige rinse". As promised, it turned her grey streaks mid-blonde, and it appeared as though Frankie's mum had golden highlights in her auburn hair. Now her cheeks were flushed, and her eyes sparkled, as she danced attendance on their unexpected visitor. Frankie sat on a chair dragged in from the kitchen, and surveyed the professor from her corner of the lounge. He reminded her of a "granddad" style doll she'd been given for her seventh birthday. The toy manufactures had simply glued a pair of glasses and a few wisps of greying hair onto an standard doll's head, and dressed it in corduroy trousers, checked shirt and a waistcoat. Professor Chown's pink skin was the same texture as newly moulded plastic. Behind his glasses, his eyes twinkled, but Frankie knew he was laughing at a private joke, and wished again that Ford hadn't left her at the garden gate, with a kiss and a promise to call her later.

Professor Chown looked directly at Frankie, but he spoke to Tony.

'So this is young Miss Shaunessy, eh? I understand your daughter had the privilege of seeing a griffin.'

Frankie squirmed, unsure if she was supposed to answer.

Moments passed when no-one spoke, then Tony said: 'A silly misunderstanding. You know what teenagers are like. That Pete Roberts will say anything to get his name in the papers.' And Tony actually chuckled, Frankie stared at him, and then smiled weakly, in response to the pleading in his eyes.

Her mum bustled back into the room carrying a tray. Frankie noticed she'd broken out the good cups and saucers, the blue willow patterns, which normally never moved from the Welsh dresser. Tony hurriedly swept all mum's paperwork to one side, as she slid the tray onto the coffee table. 'Frankie love, go and check the oven, I popped some sausage rolls in,' she smiled at Professor Chown, as if seeking his approval. Without taking his eyes from Frankie, Professor Chown told her mum he took milk and two sugars, adding 'I'd like the opportunity to talk further to your daughter about her experience, at some stage.'

Frankie bolted for the kitchen, but it wasn't until she was bending down, trying to peer through the smoked glazed door of the oven, that she realised Chown had said "griffin". Not "dragon" as the newspapers had reported, but "griffin." Pinching the hot sausage rolls directly from the oven shelf and onto a plate, Frankie started to clatter smaller plates from the cupboard, then had second thoughts. She collected the fine china tea-plates from the Welsh dresser, rinsed and dried them quickly, then transferred the sausage rolls onto a matching platter, and returned to the lounge. Tony winked, just briefly, but enough to say "thank you", as Frankie rearranged tea cups and arranged plates on the coffee table. With her sweetest smile, Frankie invited Professor Chown to help himself.

His jacket sleeves were a little too small for him, as though he'd purchased child age twelve, instead of age thirteen. They shot up as he reached for his tea, and his watch, too large for him, slipped from his wrist to his hand, giving a brief glimpse of a faded blue tattooed bracelet.

Muttering about having homework to get ready, Frankie backed out of the room. Tony reached over, and grabbed her hand, pulling her over to the sofa. Sitting beside Tony, Frankie's mum grabbed her other hand. 'Isn't this wonderful Frankie – it's like our prayers have been answered!'

Professor Chown's smile hadn't left his face, now he seemed like a beardless miniature Father Christmas, watching indulgently. 'What prayers, mum?' Frankie asked.

'The professor's been in contact with an old university friend of his, in Germany: Dr. Dawson – and he's in charge of a team of specialists in cutting edge neurology – ' 'Not only that, but he's heard all about Michael – and he thinks he can help!' Tony blurted.

Professor Chown chuckled. 'Oh, my dear Mr and Mrs Fletcher, and Miss Shaunessy, when Dr. Dawson says "he thinks he can help," believe me, your son's chances of recovery have just improved by a thousand and one percent.' Ducking his head, he sipped at his tea, peering at Frankie over the cup's rim. Tony gave a strangled gurgle, 'Please, I'm Tony, and –' '– I'm Louise!'

Frankie gave another weak smile, refrained from a curtsey, and disentangling her hands from her mum and Tony's grasp, backed out of the room. *I hope those sausage rolls give that old faker indigestion,* she thought.

Instead of going upstairs to her bedroom, Frankie sneaked out into the back garden, and scrambled over the fence into Gary's garden.

'Watcha Frankie-Mankie!' A voice called from a hammock slung between a washing line pole and the garden fence.

'Hi Gary,' Frankie wanted to add "don't call me that," but it was better than his other rhyme for "Frankie", and in any case, she wanted him in a good mood.

After offering Gary a sausage roll, Frankie leaned against the fence and casually jerked her head towards Lisa's house.

'Heard you talking to that old cow again,' she said. Gary shrugged, setting his hammock rocking slightly. 'Bally *was* chasing her cat.' He said. Frankie grimaced in reply, unwilling to excuse Lisa's behaviour for any reason. 'What's that tattoo around her wrist all about Gary?'

He shrugged again, with a mouth full of sausage roll. 'Dunno Frankie' he finally managed.

'Will you ask her, next time you see her?'

Gary twisted up from his hammock to squint at her, scratched at his bulbous nose, and then dusted pastry crumbs from his tee-shirt. 'What's the big deal Frank?' And Frankie hated that name more than any other, but forced a smile. 'No big deal Gazza – just wondering, just curious.'

He squinted at her for a bit longer, turning the crow's feet around his eyes into a crazy maze of wrinkles, before saying 'well you know what that did for the cat.'

Frankie shrugged, and with an exaggerated pout in a little girl voice said 'Please? Pretty please?' Laughing silently, Gary slumped back in his hammock, crossed his arms over his chest and said 'All right, sweetie-pie, I'll see what I can find out for you.' His eyes closed, and Frankie snuck away and climbed back into her own garden, hoping the dozey old hippy would deliver.

<<<<<*****>>>>>

For the next three days, Frankie's mum sung Professor Chown's praises, in between hugging herself and asking first Tony, then Frankie if this could be really happening.

'You've still got to get dad to agree yet,' Frankie warned. Her mum's face hardened at the mention of her ex-husband. 'Oh he will – once Michael's in Germany, he won't have to pay for the nursing home fees anymore – and that's all he's worried about.'

Frankie thought her mum was being harsh, but was probably right. Their real dad; their "biological father" had a legal obligation to continue paying for his children's upkeep until they were eighteen. *Bummer for him that Michael's upkeep included round the clock nursing.* But Frankie didn't say that out loud, although her mum would probably agree.

<<<<<*****>>>>>

Frankie's mum was right. On Saturday, she answered a knock to find Postie John on the doorstep, wanting her to sign for an envelope. Frankie also took in a parcel for their neighbour, Gary. When her mum returned from walking Bally, she pounced on the A4 stiff brown envelope, and tearing it open, she pulled out a sheaf of papers. Thumbing through to the bottom line, she shot a look of triumph in Frankie's direction.

'"*Our client, Mr Shaunessy, gives his full permission for the minor, Michael George Shaunessy, to be moved from Essex to Germany, on the understanding that he will not incur any additional costs, and furthermore, transfer of care to Badaan clinic in Germany will absolve our client of any further costs, or parental responsibility towards said minor; Michael George Shaunessy.*"'

She raised her eyebrows, waiting for Frankie to comment.

'Harry Mandleson will have to write back to dad's solicitor, and he isn't going to be happy about that last condition.' Harry Mandleson was mum's solicitor, a little terrier of a man, especially when it came to Michael's affairs.

Snarling, Frankie's mum thrust her face into Frankie's, who recoiled.

'It doesn't matter, because Michael's *going* to Germany, and Dr Dawson *will* bring him out of this coma, and we won't need *his* money anymore.' Her hands shook as she reinserted the papers into the envelope. 'I'm going down the library, I'm making copies of all this, a copy for that nursing home, and a copy for Mandleson, and then tomorrow, I'll get things rolling for Michael to be transferred.' She looked at Frankie, with a pleading expression in her eyes. 'In two years time, when you and Michael turn eighteen, you're adults in the eyes of the law, and everything changes – do you understand?'

Frankie thought she did. Mum meant that their real dad wouldn't be under any obligation to support his children financially. But two years and being eighteen was a lifetime away – surely Michael would be home by then?

'We don't know anything about this Professor Chown – how did he get to hear about Michael anyway?' Frankie kept her arms rigid at her sides, and clenched her fists, in an effort not to tear the legal documents away from her mum.

Frankie's mum glanced at the floor, then back up at Frankie, but wouldn't meet her eyes. 'He read about your escapade in the local paper, made enquiries, found out Tony was a copper, and Michael was in a nursing home. What's wrong with you anyway? Don't you *want* your brother to get better?'

Without waiting for an answer, her mum snatched up Tony's car keys, and yanking the front door open, flung herself through it, slamming the door behind. Bally whined softly, and feeling empty inside, Frankie went to open a can of dog food for him. As always, her stomach heaved, and she held her breath while setting the stinking bowl of dog's meat on the kitchen floor, for Bally to slobber over. The doorbell rang, and Frankie went to answer it, thinking mum had probably forgotten something.

'Her manners perchance?' She said out loud in a condescending voice. Instead it was a bleary eyed Gary, newly risen from last night's revelries, calling for his parcel. Looking over his shoulder Frankie spotted Chelsi and Poppy coming along the street, and collecting Gary's parcel from the chair, shoved it into his hands, eager to get rid of her frazzled looking neighbour before her friends arrived.

'Found out what Lisa's tattoo's all about!'

Frankie groaned inside, resigned to Chelsi and Poppy sniggering at Gary's puce pink dressing gown. 'Really?'

'Yeah – it's a tribal thing.'

'Tribal?'

'Our neighbour reckons she's descended from a tribe of the elite.'

Frankie jeered, 'Elite what? Pygmies?'

Gary bopped the parcel over her head, playfully. 'The Elite are "*The Elite*" – that's how they know each other – that funky tattoo around their wrists.' Giving a cheery wave to Chelsi and Poppy, he retreated back into his own house. *Thank you god!* Frankie thought, swinging the door open wider for her friends to enter the house. Her mind wanted to delve deeper into the information Gary had wheedled from Lisa, the word "Elite" had set off tiny chimes. But the warning bells were distant enough to be dismissed easily, and in any case, Frankie wanted to get out the house before mum came back.

Chelsi wore burgundy hot pants over thick black leggings, while Poppy wore a short red skirt over black and white patterned leggings. Compared to them, Frankie looked terribly ordinary in her jeans, but she wasn't worried. She wasn't seeing Ford this weekend. He would be training today. Tomorrow he wanted to visit the shopping mall for some last minute essentials, before travelling up north to take up City's training offer. Frankie wished she could go shopping with him. But Tony and her mum were visiting Michael, and someone had to walk Bally and Frankie had promised to get dinner started too. But meanwhile, her girls were here and they planned to go into town, and Frankie decided she was going to have a brilliant Saturday.

<<<<<*****>>>>>

The phone rang four times on Sunday. First it was Professor Chown's secretary, telling Frankie (not asking), that Professor Chown would be calling on them later that night, around eight o'clock and to make certain the whole family could attend the great man. The next two callers wanted to talk to the head of the household, so Frankie placed the phone handset next to Bally, and encouraged him to bark. Finally Ford rang, to say he'd managed to get tickets to see James Bond that night.

'I'm so sorry Ford, I can't. This professor man's coming round to talk about Michael, and he wants the whole family present.' There was a silence, and Frankie could sense Ford frowning, and felt impatient with him.

'I'm sorry, I can't come out tonight' she said, and hung up, thinking Ford had a cheek anyway, and should have checked with her first. Although she knew that was childish, she'd been rattling on about the new James Bond movie for weeks.

To her annoyance, apart from asking Frankie if she'd seen any griffins lately, Professor Chown ignored the teenager, and went into a huddle with her mum and Tony. Frankie prepared her school books and lunch ready for Monday morning. Then she had a bath, using all the hot water, and slunk off to bed. She didn't wish any of the adults goodnight. She did send a last "goodnight" text to Ford. He hadn't responded by the time she turned off her nightlight at nine-fifteen, and Frankie supposed he was watching the exploits of 007, and wondered who he'd invited to the cinema in her place.

Laying in bed, Frankie wondered again about Chown. The Professor was the only person, apart from Balkind's Rider to use the term "griffin" rather than "dragon." She chewed at a fingernail, thinking of the hungry expression on the professor's face at the mention of the word "griffin." *It doesn't matter, they've made it back to their own world,* she told herself, and winced as her teeth tore into a cuticle. *At least, I hope they've made it back into their own world, and in any case, I hope to God the Rider and Balkind never run into Professor Weirdo.*

Chapter fifteen.

Another Monday morning, another English lesson. Girls clustered around Chelsi's desk, to admire her new acrylic fingernails. Though it was nine-fifteen, they were still teacher-less, and Frankie allowed herself to hope that Miss Gerraty's absence meant she'd been transferred to another school. Poppy too was either late or absent today; Ford wouldn't be returning to school until after Easter, and then just for exam purposes. Frankie looked down at her own nails; which she kept short for keyboard practice. *Maybe I could get away with a French manicure.*

Annette's shrill voice shattered her musing: 'Daniel Craig's so cool! I was clutching Ford's arm all through the film like crazy ...'

'Ford Henderson asked *you* out?' Chelsi's upper lip curled, and she stared at Annette. Frankie sensed heads craning towards her, and the room became stifling, but she continued to inspect her nails. 'Well, Frankie couldn't go – could you Frankie?' Annette cooed. Frankie hid her face in her schoolbag, pretending to be hunting for a pen in her school bag, while she scrabbled through putdowns in her mind. Finally she managed 'I couldn't be bothered. Ford must have been really desperate to ask you out.'

'Ohhh, bitch!' Perminda's dark eyes lit up with malice. Detaching herself from Chelsi's admirers, Annette swaggered over to Frankie's desk. 'Desperate to get away from your whining – Ford said he was sick to death of your mum's nagging too!'

Behind Annette's shoulder, Chelsi bit her lip, looking dismayed. At that instant everyone quietened, as the door handle turned, and Miss Gerraty walked into the classroom, followed by Poppy. Miss Gerraty clapped her hands:

'Back to your seats please everyone! Paul – out here and spit that chewing gum into the waste paper basket! Stuart Pearson – sit down now! Really – I expect better from Year 11 – you're sixteen year olds, not six.'

Annette poked her tongue out at Frankie, and scuttled back to her own desk. Chelsi mouthed "duh!" at Frankie, before turning to face the front, as Poppy slipped into the seat beside her. Paul Kastel mooched back to his desk, chewing-gumless.

Miss Gerraty stacked a pile of familiar grubby textbooks on the front desk of each aisle. Chelsi took the top textbook, and twisted to pass the remainder back to Frankie. "What the hell?!" She mouthed, but Frankie ignored her, slipped a textbook off the pile for herself, and passed the rest back to Perminda, avoiding her eyes too.

"What the hell!" – Chelsi was right – what was Ford playing at? *I should have gone out with him last night, I'm sure he only asked Annette because he didn't want to waste the tickets.* She thought, worrying a strand of hair between her teeth.

'Francesca Shaunessy – take your hair out of your mouth! Were you paying attention?!'

If she said yes, she'd be ask to repeat Miss Gerraty's instructions, if she said no, then everyone would guess at her confusion.

'Sorry miss, Perminda was asking me if I had a spare pen.' Frankie said, crossing her fingers and sighing with relief when Perminda backed her up. 'Sorry miss, mine ran out just now.'

'In future, make certain you come prepared and bring a spare pen into my class.' Miss Gerraty crossed her arms, and perched on the oversized teacher's desk. 'Poppy has come up with an excellent suggestion. Year 12 are going to put on a play as part of their English coursework, and this will count towards your exam results.'

Frankie hunched her shoulders, *please not Romeo and Juliet*, she begged of the universe.

'We're going to stage *Romeo and Juliet*,' Miss Gerraty continued, and then paused; Frankie's groan went unnoticed, as excited murmurs swept through the class. Most of them would rather do anything than written work. 'We'll be aiming to perform at Christmas – I know that's only two months' away – but we've got half term to rehearse in between – Shakespeare's players learned their lines in a week – however, we will have to get cracking on this.'

Frankie slumped into her seat, crossing her fingers and hoping for the least active lady-in-waiting part, or better still, a scullery maid.

It seemed that Miss Gerraty, along with Poppy, had already decided on Chelsi for the leading female role. Chelsi blushed even deeper when Max Harley, class geek, was pencilled in as Romeo. 'Now, nothing's cut and dried yet. Roles can change.' Miss Gerraty's eyes flickered between the notes she held in her hand and her students, as she announced the speaking roles. 'The rest of you will be either Montagues, or Capulets, but don't forget, things can change. So you should all be reading along, and trying to memorise as much of the play as possible.' She glanced at her wrist watch, just as the recess bell rang. The class buzzed with excitement again, for once, Miss Gerraty didn't tell them to be quiet. Perched on her desk, she encouraged suggestions, listening and nodding and adding her own comments.

Four desks behind Frankie, Annette announced loudly 'What a shame Ford won't be here. He could have played Romeo.'

Frankie decided it was time to leave. She leaned over to collect her bag, and then straightened up ready to bolt for the door, but she'd left it too late. Calling the class to order with a single clap of her hands, Miss Gerraty dismissed them for break. Annette and Chardonnay were first out of the door, walking with their heads together, whispering and giggling. Without waiting for her usual girls, Chelsi followed Annette with determined steps. Max trailed behind Chelsi, with a bemused look on his face, as though shell shocked at his good luck.

Frankie hung back, letting her classmates bundle out into the corridor before her. She didn't want to answer any silly questions about her and Ford, and she suspected Annette might be lingering in the corridor, ready with another barbed comment. Now she'd left her escape too late again.

'Not you Francesca – Poppy and I need to discuss something with you. Go and sit back in your seat.' Miss Gerraty closed the door behind the last student as she spoke. Frankie shot a startled glance in Poppy's direction, and feeling too bemused to protest, she slunk back to her chair. Miss Gerraty followed Frankie across the room, and perched on Chelsi's desk, next to Poppy, her new pet. Poppy swivelled around in her seat to face Frankie, and seemed to be hugging a secret to herself. Shakespeare once said that names didn't matter, a rose by any other name would smell as sweet. Which was just as well, because no-one could look less like a 'poppy' than Poppy. Her hair was plaited into a long dark whip, and her eyes, also dark, seemed to peer out above high Slavic cheekbones. She resembled a mischievous imp, not a 'poppet', and Frankie was sometimes in awe of her sharp tongue.

'Did you hear me, Francesca?' Miss Gerraty asked.

Frankie gulped at Poppy, wondering what she'd missed. Poppy grinned, 'I told Miss Gerraty that you can play the piano.'

'Poppy will be our director, if you can provide the musical interludes, or rather, incidental music – then it will be a purely student produced play.'

'Me? You want me to provide the play's music?'

'Yes! I, that is, Miss Gerraty and me thought it would be great if you could play Tchaikovsky's Symphony.'

Frankie gulped again. *She* thought it would be great if she could play Tchaikovsky's symphony.

'I can't ... I'm nowhere near good enough – Tchaikovsky's Symphony Number Six –' in her mind, she heard the opening chords of the great man's composition for Romeo and Juliet, and quivered inside.

'I can't – and that's that!' Even to her own ears, she sounded sulky.

Reaching out, Poppy twirled a strand of Frankie's hair around her fingers, and yanked it. 'Dork! We're not asking for the whole symphony – even I know you'd need at least half an orchestra for that! Miss Gerraty's going to ask Miss Worstall to work on a ....' She broke off, and squinted up at Miss Gerraty, 'what did you call it – bits and pieces – like a melody?'

Frankie's mind snatched at the piano's part in the famous symphony, her fingers stroked over the wooden desktop, and she nodded her head involuntarily. Before she could stop herself, she said 'It might work –'

'It will work, and it will count towards your grades.' Miss Gerraty straightened up from the desk, 'that's settled then. I'll speak to Miss Worstall, I'm sure you'll be able to use the school's piano to practise at lunch times, and of course during music and some English lessons.'

Frankie gulped for the third time – how had this happened? Poppy grinned, and said 'Don't look so worried – you'll be fine!' With one of her quick darting movements, she stooped to collect Frankie's school bag, and clutching her own notes, jerked her head towards the door 'Come on, or we'll be late for our next lesson.'

Frankie grimaced, wondering if anyone would notice if she skipped her next lesson. She and her one time best friend, Annette were the only two girls from her original form taking History for one of their exams.

Frankie *was* late; but Mr Walters simply gave a welcoming smile, and continued enthusing over his favourite Victorian.

'Everyone laughed at Brunel, when the first sewers were laid down in London, and do you know why they laughed?' He rocked to and fro on the balls of his feet, and pointed at Simon Bishop, who shrugged and mumbled 'dunno sir.'

Mr Walters aimed his forefinger at Max Harley who promptly said: 'Because the sewer pipes were large enough for a man to stand upright in, but only carried a trickle of waste.'

'Exactly!' Beaming, he turned to the whiteboard, and wrote in large block letters "FORESIGHT."

'Brunel had foresight – he knew that the population of London would increase dramatically over the next generation – and the generation after that. But how do we get foresight?' Several hands shot up, the answer was a mantra for Mr Walters. 'With hindsight.' The class chanted.

'Right again! If you want to read the future; study history!'

Frankie tuned out the teacher's gravelly voice, she wasn't that interested in London's sewerage system. She glanced furtively towards Annette, puzzled by her one-time friend's subdued manner. As though feeling Frankie's eyes on her, Annette raised her head, and sneered. A red mark glowed on her left cheek, and Frankie wondered if Chelsi had had more than "words" with Annette. Frankie's phone vibrated against her chest, and keeping an eye on Mr Walters, she sneaked it from her inner blazer pocket. Holding the phone under the desk, she saw she had a text from Ford and opened it.

"Sorry about last night. Maybe it's for the best. Stay cool Frankie. I'll catch up with you around Christmas time" she read. Frankie's eyes skimmed the text again, and then she started, almost jumping from her seat, as a hand snatched the mobile phone from her.

'No texting in my class. You can have it back when the last bell rings.' Mr Walters turned the phone off, and slipped it into the pocket of his corduroy jacket as he walked back to his desk. Frankie clutched the edge of her seat, locking her ankles around each other to stop herself from chasing after him and snatching the phone back – *I've been dumped! Ford's dumped me – was it something Annette said to him last night? Or is it something I've done? Or does he just want to concentrate on his football?*

She glanced round the room again. Everyone else was scribbling notes into their exercise books from the whiteboard, and Mr Walters watched her, with a slightly puzzled look on his face. With an apologetic smile, Frankie uncapped one of her pens, and began jotting down notes, trying to catch up with her classmates.

<<<<<*****>>>>>

At last the bell rang for lunch time. In spite of Frankie's begging and pleading, mum still made her take a packed lunch into school. ("No telling what goes into those school dinners," her mum had said darkly, buttering wholemeal slices of bread, and reaching into the fridge for a packet of organic cheese). So Frankie sat alone on the playground bench, waiting for Chelsi and Poppy to finish their lunch and come outside. There was a lead weight inside her stomach, and she didn't even unwrap her sandwiches, knowing she'd never force them past the lump in her throat. After an age of waiting, the school doors swung open, and students began wandering into the playground.

Summer Wilson and Poppy headed towards Frankie; 'Chelsi's been sent home!' Poppy announced, plonking herself down next to Frankie. 'Sent home? Why?' Frankie gasped.

'Because of you!' Summer answered for Poppy, who frowned and said 'Don't blame Frankie!' But she swept a hand over Summer's punkish orange hair cut to take the sting out of her words, and Summer grinned, to show she wasn't serious. But by now the bench was surrounded by other Year 11 girls, and most of them were only too keen to blame Frankie.

'Why not – it *is* all her fault!'

'Yeah – you don't want Ford, but you don't want anyone else to have him.' Joy Lewis stooped to thrust her long face into Frankie's.

'Oh shut up, you horse-faced old mare.' Poppy said, and linking her arm through Frankie's, stood up and dragging Frankie with her, walked away from the bench, heading towards the school, with Summer following. Whispers started up, and Frankie heard the word "Witch" again.

'Take no notice, Annette's been asking for it for a long time now. Smug little cow.' Raising her voice Poppy said 'And if Joy Lewis and Karen McGregor don't watch their mouths, they'll have a good smack too.'

'Damn straight!' Summer agreed.

Frankie tried to smile, but it seemed everyone was whispering and pointing at her again. This time there was no Ford to come to her rescue.

Frankie spent a miserable afternoon moping, and was lucky to escape having detention – as if she cared! Was Ford really sick of her? Had he dumped her for Annette? He was leaving for Manchester tomorrow, at the crack of dawn. *I'll go around his house after school. He should at least talk to me face to face,* she decided. But Cynthia, the nicer of the school secretaries was waiting outside the classroom after Frankie's last lesson, to tell Frankie she was wanted by the school's principal.

'Sorry Francesca, but Miss Prater wants to get to the bottom of an incident that happened during first break.'

Frankie slopped along the corridor in the wake of Cynthia's broad frame, wondering idly where Cynthia managed to buy mini-skirts to cover her huge backside. She had plenty of time to think about that, and other things while she waited in the narrow corridor outside of Miss Prater's office. She heard laughter, and Poppy's voice, and tried to listen closer. The door opened suddenly, Poppy's face peered out, and she pulled Frankie inside the principal's tiny office.

Miss Prater's face beamed. 'Francesca – Poppy tells me Year 11 has a special treat in store for the whole school for Christmas.' Her eyes sparkled, and her lips glistened, as though she'd been licking them repeatedly. It seemed Chelsi and Annette were forgotten. It was impossible not to be caught up with Miss Prater and Poppy's enthusiasm for the forth coming production, and when the two girls finally left Miss Prater's office, they found the school corridors deserted; apart from a solitary cleaner sweeping a broom from side to side in a menacing fashion.

'Oh no, my phone!' Frankie struck her forehead, and began running for the staff room, hoping to catch Mr Walters.

'Frankie – I've got to go, see you tomorrow!' Poppy called over her shoulder, hurrying away in the opposite direction. Frankie knocked on the Staff Room door, and after waiting five minutes, tried the handle. As she'd suspected, it was locked. Puffing out her fringe again, she turned, and began walking for the exit. *I'll go straight round Ford's house, I deserve more than a text – if he wants to cool things for a while, that's okay, but he should at least tell me face to face.* Frankie told herself for the millionth time that day, trying not to think of what she'd do if Ford refused open the door to her.

She never got the chance to find out. Tony's Vauxhall waited outside the school gates, parked on double yellow lines. Normally his face softened at the sight of her, but now the worry lines deepened across his brow, and Frankie knew she was in trouble. She climbed into the passenger's seat and slammed the door closed, thankful none of the other kids were around to see her being picked up from school like a Year 7 baby. She buckled her seat belt hurriedly, willing Tony to drive off.

'What do you think you're playing at young lady? Your mum's been trying to text you since four o'clock – she's going mad with worry!' He said nothing about being hauled out of bed, and made to go out hunting for her.
'Sorry Tony, I'm sorry – Mr Walters confiscated my phone.'

'That's no excuse – you shouldn't be using it during lessons. Wait till your mum gets home – this is the third time in less than two months – that phone's only for keeping contact with us anyway!' Frankie turned to stare out of the window, and tuned Tony's ranting out. She didn't care if she was grounded for the rest of her life. Nothing anyone could say or do could possibly make her life any more miserable.

Chapter sixteen.

The cell measured five paces by seven: the Rider had walked its perimeter many times. His furniture consisted of a thin mattress on the floor. He had grown used to the smell of stale air and his own body odour.

Twice a day, they came for him. The routine never varied. His jailers would allow him to use the bathroom, then take him into another room for questioning.

This room was larger, and bright with artificial lights. The Rider did not know for sure, but supposed they were still underground. The room smelled clean, with an overpowering scent of pine. After the first three visits, the merest whiff of pine made him want to gag. Professor Chown waited in this room, along with an assistant, a woman with dark hair and gold bangles around her wrists.

A black leather chair also waited for him. Behind the chair stood a metal trough full of water. After the guards had strapped the Rider into the chair, Chown's assistant attached wires to his wrists and chest with a sticky material. The woman surveyed him as she worked, examining his body as though he were an animal in her care. Her bangles jangled against his nerves, clinking in time to her deft movements. He kept his eyes averted until footsteps told him the assistant had settled herself behind her workstation. At this point, the guards usually left the room.

Then the questioning would begin.

He told them over and over again that the girl had called and Balkind had simply responded. Somehow they knew he told the truth.

He told them over and over again that he didn't know the girl's name. Somehow they knew he lied, and the torture commenced. Sometimes it continued until blackness engulfed him, and he woke to find himself in the cell once more.

This last session had been the worst. Only the woman, Dr Perry, had been present, and seemed determined to extract information from him. She so badly wanted to please her master, Professor Chown on his return from London. During that session, the Rider experienced what it would be like to drown four times.

He might have slept for only an hour, or seven hours, or seven nights. He had no way of knowing. But when he woke up, he made a decision: The next time they tipped the chair back, and immersed his head in water, he would gulp the water into his lungs.

At least they don't know about the girl, he comforted himself, as he went about the routine he had set for himself. He shook out the blanket that covered him at night, smoothed the sheet over the thin mattress, before refolding the blanket and placing it on top of his pillow. With nothing else to do, he sat down on the mattress, crossed his legs and waited.

He had already examined the cell minutely, several times over. The large metal door at the far end was the only way in or out. It took the guards almost a minute to unlock all the bolts, and the older guard always grunted as he pushed the door open. The Rider fell into a daydream, in which he managed to overpower both guards, and escape this prison. Since both guards appeared very capable of taking care of themselves, and the Rider, though taller, was much slighter in build, it would only ever be a daydream to while away the boredom. *Rather than swimming, I should have tried to escape before I was imprisoned in this cell,* he berated himself.

His stomach began to complain. A meagre ration of biscuits and cheese *always* arrived shortly after he woke up, but not this morning. He yearned for the taste of hot sweet tea; although as time dragged on and his thirst became unbearable, he would have settled for a mouthful of water. Now images of the lakes and waterfalls of the Delphia mountains invaded his mind. He pushed them away quickly.

The day dragged on and on. His stomach cramped with emptiness, and his tongue swelled until it was too large for his mouth. But he could cope with hunger and thirst. What drove him almost crazy was the need to visit the bathroom. Just as he'd convinced himself there was no shame in getting up, and walking over to a corner to relieve himself, another unwanted thought struck him. *What if no one ever comes for me?* Stunned, he flumped onto the mattress, and lay prostrate on his back. He forgot about hunger, thirst, and even the pressing need to pee, as he considered the nightmarish prospect of rotting in this cell.

This is my punishment, a just punishment too, for failing Balkind. Although griffins could survive without food for much longer than any other animal, by now even the well nourished Balkind would be feeling hungry. Over the next seven days, starvation would surely set in, and Balkind would suffer a slow painful death. Of course, dying of thirst wouldn't be any easier, but it would at least be quicker. However, the chalk cavern where Balkind waited had its own underground lake. Balkind might emerge from his hiding place deep within the Chiltern Hills, when he could no longer bear the hunger pangs. What would happen to the griffin then could only be imagined.

The Rider gritted his teeth. He had done all he could. He decided he could die with honour, or at least, without shame. He would simply lay here until death claimed him.

He must have fallen into an uneasy sleep, for the door pushing open woke him.

It was Shaf; the turban-wearing guard and the nicer of the two, who entered carrying a tray. Shaking off his fugue, the Rider sat up. Immediately a slash of pain ripped across his lower stomach, and he bent double, clutching his waist.

Shaf understood. He shook his head at the Rider's obstinacy, then dragged him to his feet, and along the corridor to the bathroom.

'Kid, you might think you're proving a point, but the only dude you're hurting is yourself. Get me?'

The Rider merely groaned, not minding when Shaf left the bathroom door open to ensure he didn't escape through the sewer pipe or something equally impossible. But it seemed his guard wanted to talk:

'We found the girl you know," he said. "Found her ages ago. The professor's been playing games with you, while trying to work on an angle to go at the Shaunessy family.' Lowering his voice he whispered, 'Dr Perry even got a job at the kid's school …'

The Rider paused in the middle of washing his hands, and cast a backwards glance over his shoulder. Shaf nodded.

'She managed to dig up all kinds of dirt – did you know your girl's brother has been at death's door for the past two years?'

The Rider frowned. Was he being taunted? But Shaf spoke in a low voice, and seemed troubled for some reason. He turned around and, scooping water from the wash-hand basin, splashed it over his face.

Shaf continued. 'The old man's convinced the girl's mother he can cure the brother. They're already putty in his hands – ready to do anything he asks.'

The Rider frowned again, Balkind would almost certainly answer Francesca's calling, even after all this time. Once Professor Chown captured the griffin, what would happen next? Patting his face and hands dry, the Rider straightened and turned around.

'Tell the professor I should be present when the girl summons the griffin. He hasn't eaten for over three weeks. He will be hungry, frightened, and very very angry.'

The Sikh nodded. 'I'll tell him. Come on, hurry up – we haven't got all day,' he injected a harsher tone into his voice, just as his colleague stomped down the basement stairs and loomed into view. The older man's head and neck were flushed pink, and the wasp tattooed on the side of his neck appeared to buzz with irritation.

Dropping his head, the Rider meekly complied, shuffling his way along the corridor and back to his cell. Wheels spun in his mind. If the professor allowed him outside, given even the slightest chance for escape, he would take it.

Chapter seventeen.

Around four hundred pupils crowded into the assembly hall, from Year 7's to Year 10's. Some sixth formers and a smattering of Year 11's lurked at the back; most were taking part in the play. Frankie shuffled her sheet music on the piano stand, and readjusted the stool, as teachers guided Year 8's into third and fourth row seats. The front two rows were already filled with Year 7's, who giggled and chattered, dizzy with their freedom from lessons, and the nearness of Christmas.

Mr Sharky's voice rang out 'Waddle and Greenson! One more peep from either of you, and I'll assume both of you would rather be in my classroom for the next two hours!' In the absolute silence that followed he added 'If there's anyone else in the hall who'd rather be doing maths – speak up now!'

Frankie grinned. For once, Mr Sharky's sarcasm was welcome. *This'll be an easy audience, they'll applaud anything, rather than face old Sarky!* The past two months had passed by in a whirl of rehearsals; Poppy and Chelsi had fallen out with each other a dozen times, Max Harley had transformed from class nerd into a hunk, and Paul Kastel had declared he was going to audition for a stage school. Frankie had spent the majority of her lunch hours learning how little she knew about music, and trying desperately to perfect her piano playing. She stifled a yawn. Poppy had insisted that everyone involved in the play should arrive at school by seven am. When Frankie had protested, "I'm not on stage, and I don't need to "dress up"", Chelsi rounded on her. 'You're part of this play, and you are "dressing up" – or do you want Annette to have one of the prettier outfits?"

It was now nine twenty, and Frankie had been awake since five this morning. She stroked the silky folds of the gown she wore. Chelsi and Poppy's gowns were tighter fitting, with medieval style bodices and long trailing sleeves. Frankie's sapphire blue gown was more contemporary, with a sweet heart neckline and puffy off the shoulder short sleeves. Perminda had styled Frankie's hair, pulling it back with a tiara decorated with imitation flowers of blue, and she felt like a bridesmaid at a posh wedding.

The curtains billowed, and Poppy appeared on stage. Her peach coloured gown swept the floor, and chestnut ringlets bounced around her shoulders. A quiet murmuring broke out, and then lessened to the odd whisper. Poppy looked around the hall, waiting for complete quiet. Then, with a brief nod in Frankie's direction, Poppy began her narration. As she spoke the now familiar lines, Frankie began to play, very softly. Although she'd learned the chords by heart, she kept her eyes on the musical score. Miss Worstall's simple arrangement of Tchaikovsky's symphony number six flowed seamlessly; the bitter sweet melodies gave a foretaste of the impending doom awaiting. Poppy finished 'What here shall miss, our toil shall strive to mend' with a flourish, and Frankie eased her foot off the piano's left pedal, allowing the exquisite notes to swell throughout the hall. The curtains swung open revealing the actors on stage at the precise moment Frankie finished playing. She grinned at Miss Worstall when a voice called out 'that's the music from one of Disney's films!'

The play galloped along. Poppy stood at Frankie's side to manage the stage directions and ready to prompt any forgetful actors. Once or twice she had to nudge Frankie into playing the incidental music. Along with the rest of the school, Frankie watched spellbound, forgetting even that Max and Chelsi were only pretending to be Romeo and Juliet – a heart rendering love story was playing out in front of her eyes and Frankie sensed the entire audience willing the next scene to begin.

There were gasps of 'No,' and 'she isn't dead, she's sleeping' as Romeo sobbed over Juliet's lifeless form. When he drew his dagger and raised it high in the air before plunging it into his chest, a deathly quiet smothered the hall. Seconds later Juliet sat up, stretched, and yawned. A voice called out 'You stupid cow, why didn't you wake up before?!' followed by a scuffle and the main door creaking open as the heckler was thrown out. Juliet's head bent way over Romeo's chest, her long blonde hair shielding both their faces. Somehow Frankie knew that Chelsi's shoulders shook with giggles, rather than sobs. She stroked the piano keys beneath her fingers, and cringed, as she waited for the whole school to latch on and explode with laughter. Then with a flash of inspiration, Frankie played a sequence of chords. She sensed her audience listening as they struggled to recognise the familiar intro; so she played them again, and after a moment's pause, swept into a rendition of Leonard Cohen's Hallelujah. This time she carried the audience with her, as she poured her heart into her music.

Poppy, who had been nibbling her lip, beamed at Frankie. When she judged the audience had once more been lured back into the moment, Frankie allowed the notes to die away. Juliet snatched up Romeo's dagger, and angling it towards her own chest spoke, shattering the renewed silence.

As the curtains began to close, Poppy gathered the loose folds of her gown with one hand, and bounded back on stage to deliver the epilogue.

The curtains opened again, revealing the full cast lined across the stage, standing hand in hand. Teachers seated along the side aisles of the hall began applauding, then the lower years in the front rows joined in, until finally everyone was slapping their hands together. Frankie's eardrums throbbed and she put her hands over her ears, surprised to find her face was burning. If this was success, Frankie wasn't sure she liked it.

Chelsi and Max were thrust forward to take centre stage; they took a deep bow. As Chelsi straightened upright, she held out her arms in Frankie's direction, motioning her to come up onstage. Luckily, the piano was right next to the hall's fire exit – even luckier, the audience, glad of an excuse to stamp and cheer rose to their feet like a Mexican wave – giving Frankie the chance to leg it out the hall and into the playground.

She bolted head down, heading for the water fountain, and ran smack into her English teacher. 'Miss Gerraty!'

What was she doing out here? Why wasn't she inside with the other teachers? With vice like fingers, Miss Gerraty grasped Frankie's upper arms. When Frankie took an involuntary step backwards, her grip tightened. Before Frankie could protest or shake her off, Miss Gerraty said 'You have to come with me now – your parents need you at home.' Frankie's heart beat double time – why was she needed at home suddenly? Unless … either mum or Tony had been rushed to hospital!

She heard her name being called again, Poppy and Chelsi had followed her into the playground. Breaking free of Miss Gerraty's grip, Frankie waved an arm impatiently behind her.

'What do you mean – I have to go with you?'

'Michael's being transferred to Germany, today. You're wanted at home, now.'

Frankie's heart beat returned to normal. Poppy and Chelsi came running up, and she grinned at them, dizzy with relief.

'I have to go – Miss Gerraty's taking me home – Michael's being transferred today!'

'No! You can't!' Poppy exclaimed, but Chelsi's eyes shone, 'don't be selfish Poppy. Of course Frankie has to go. Miss Worstall can play the piano for tonight's performance.'

'What about Ford?!' Poppy demanded, 'you're not only letting me down, you're letting him down – he's come home especially to watch this play – I'm not the one being selfish – you are!'

Frankie recoiled; thankfully, Chelsi shoved Poppy aside. 'Frankie's brother comes before your play!'

With a grimace to show her distain of schoolgirl dramatics, Miss Gerraty said 'Of course Michael comes first. Now hurry up Francesca – I don't have all day,' and she ushered Frankie across the playground towards the staff car-park.

Poppy didn't give up. Clutching her skirts in one hand, she hurried to get in front of Frankie and Miss Gerraty. 'Frankie – you can't – don't do this – you're going to ruin everything.' Poppy's eyes pleaded with Frankie's.

'I wasn't supposed to tell you this – but someone from the London School of Music is coming tonight, to listen to you play – it's your big chance Frankie!' Poppy walked backwards, as she entreated her friend to stay. As they neared the playground gates, Poppy's heel caught on the hem of her gown, and she stumbled, flumping onto her backside. Miss Gerraty sidestepped Poppy, without a sideways glance, and hauled Frankie into the staff car park.

'Miss Gerraty – let go of me – Poppy –'

'Poppy will be just fine. Or is she more important to you than your brother?'

Frankie stopped struggling, and climbed meekly into Miss Gerraty's yellow Mini. Michael needed her.

Chapter eighteen.

Miss Gerraty's bracelets jangled, sliding up and down her wrist as she operated the gear stick and negotiated the roundabout, then indicated to turn left into Church Road.

Glancing down, Frankie glimpsed blue ink under the thick gold bangles. They were passing the entrance to Black Jack's Common now, and Miss Gerraty slowed and indicated to turn right.

'How do you know where I live, Miss?' Frankie asked. Miss Gerraty could have obtained Frankie's address from one of the school secretaries, but she had driven here without hesitation, as though the route was familiar to her.

'Your dad told me to turn right opposite the common, and look out for a silver Vauxhall car.' Miss Gerraty pulled up outside Frankie's house as she spoke, parking behind a large black people carrier. She turned off the ignition, and swung herself from the mini with the grace of a cat walk model. Frankie struggled to extract her legs from under the fullness of her ball gown, finally she hitched it up over her knees and half fell, half clambered out of the car. Something else troubled her about Miss Gerraty too, but she couldn't quite put her finger on it – maybe the way she'd said "Michael" so casually, or was it something to do with those bangles?

Frankie stumbled to the kerb, brushing down the full skirt of her gown, and collided with a youth wearing a brown hoodie. He stood awkwardly on the pavement, with his hands behind his back.

'Watch it!' She said rudely, embarrassed at her clumsiness. From within the hood's shadow, blue eyes stared down at her.

'I see your costume has improved, but not your manners.' The Rider said. Frankie let out a cry of surprise, and stumbled backwards.

'Shaf, get him into the people carrier – Dave – you drive Ruby's car – Ruby – bring the girl.'

Frankie looked on, astonished. A turban wearing Sikh hustled the Rider away, and Professor Chown strolled towards her, followed closely by Tony, who clutched a briefcase under his arm.

'Just a minute, not so fast.' Tony called – 'I'm having a word with Frankie first.' His face was puckered with worry, behind him the front door swung wide open; a muddle of paperwork and files littered the hall's floor.

'Tony – I don't understand – what's he doing here?' Frankie glanced at the professor, dressed in what might have passed for "casual clothing" back in the swinging sixties. His fake silk spotted cravat and pale blue blouse style jacket gave him the appearance of a Thunderbirds' puppet.

From the corner of her eye, Frankie saw the Rider being bundled into the rear of the people carrier, and the Sikh, (Shaf?) slid the door closed, and climbed into the driver's seat.

'This is a big day for you and Michael!' Professor Chown answered for Tony: 'You get to call for a griffin, and your brother gets his transfer to Germany.'

'Call for a griffin – what are you on about?!' Frankie shouted. Tony elbowed Chown out of the way, and placed his hands on Frankie's shoulders, dipping his face down to peer into hers. 'Frankie love, you don't have to do this if you don't want to … It's just that – '

' – Your mother is at your brother's bedside now. As soon as you call for the griffin, I'll confirm everything – and your brother's rehabilitation begins.'

Frankie's stomach churned, and she swallowed hard. 'Call the griffin? Are you mad?'

With a pitying smile at her childish blustering, Chown pulled a smart phone from his pocket, and clicked play. Barely visible on the miniature screen, a dark shape flitted across a darker sky, trailing a struggling figure from its talons. Seconds later the same dark shape loomed back into view, flying over a second figure jumping and punching the air with triumph.

Frankie looked at Tony; he was still staring at Chown's smart phone screen, transfixed by the image of Frankie, frozen mid air as the video clip ran out. Tony's eyes met hers, and for the first time ever, he seemed uncertain what to do, or what to say.

'Professor Chown tells me he just wants you to call for this griffin, this beast …' Tony's voice trailed off, and abruptly, he placed an arm around Frankie, hugging her tightly to his chest. The smell of dry cleaning fluids lingered around his best suit jacket, mingling with the scent of citrus soap Tony always used.

'I'm sorry Professor Chown, I can't agree to this. Frankie's mum wouldn't allow it, and I'm not going to allow it.'

Chown's face hardened, and he held out his phone to Tony. 'Then go ahead – call your wife, and tell her she won't be taking that flight to Germany after all. Michael won't get his treatment, because you don't trust me with your daughter, even with Frankie's teacher accompanying us.'

Miss Gerraty placed a hand on Tony's arm, and said calmly:

'Mr Fletcher, Francesca will be completely safe with me, and Professor Chown of course. You've seen the video. The professor has waited his whole life to see a griffin with his own eyes. We'll travel down to Essex behind you – this won't take more than an hour, I promise I won't let Francesca out of my sight.'

'What if this griffin doesn't exist – you've fallen for some sort of hoax?' Tony asked, but his grip loosened from around Frankie's shoulders, and he allowed Miss Gerraty to ease her from his grasp.

'Michael's treatment goes ahead, of course. Let Francesca come with us, to the Chiltern Hills, and call out for the griffin. Just to humour an old man?' Professor Chown pleaded.

Frankie watched as Tony rubbed the back of his neck, and glanced from Miss Gerraty, to the professor. She wanted to weep for him. Summoning up a smile, she said 'don't worry, I'll be fine, tell mum I'll see her soon. Come on then professor, Miss Gerraty – we'd better get going before it gets dark.'

She had wondered why Tony didn't simply insist on going with them. Now she realised from the manner he nursed the briefcase under his arm that it contained valuable paperwork; probably passports and almost certainly her "real" dad's consent for Michael to be transferred from England to Germany. No doubt her mum had dropped everything at Professor Chown's phone call, and hurried straight from work to Michael's side, leaving Tony to follow with the paperwork – not knowing Chown planned to place Tony in an impossible position.

Tony clutched her arm again, his blue eyes searching her face. 'So it's true then – this ... griffin does exist – and that young man in there' he jerked his head towards the people carrier 'is a visitor from another world?'

Frankie nodded, and smiled again. 'Yes, the griffin exists. They saved me. Pete Roberts and his mate attacked me over the common, and they came to my rescue.'

Professor Chown chuckled. 'So you see, my dear Tony, Francesca is among friends.' Tony shot him a look of distaste. With a quick movement, he thrust his head and hand into the Mini's open window, and snatched the keys from the ignition. Jammed behind the steering wheel, Chown's man wasn't quick enough to stop Tony, but shouted 'Hey – give those back!'

Tony tucked the keys into his jacket pocket. 'He stays here – with her car.' He indicated Miss Gerraty. 'You get the keys back when you arrive at the nursing home, with my daughter.' He took a step forward, towering over Professor Chown. 'If she isn't at that nursing home by three o'clock this afternoon, I'll have every police force in the country searching for her – and you.' He smiled grimly. 'And you better pray they find you before I do.'

Professor Chown returned Tony's glare with a smug smile. 'Help Francesca into the car, Ruby.' He held out his hand to Tony, for a handshake. 'You have my word, as a gentleman.' Frankie felt Miss Gerraty's hand in the small of her back, pushing her into the people carrier. She gathered up her skirts, and ducking her head, clambered inside the vehicle, so she never knew if Tony shook hands with the professor or not. Miss Gerraty climbed into the front bench seat next to the driver, Shaf. Seconds later the passenger door swung open, the professor jumped on board next to Miss Gerraty; Shaf started the engine, and pulled away. *I hope Tony remembers to shut the front door,* Frankie thought absently. Then another thought struck her – she twisted to face the Rider. His arms disappeared behind his back, and he sat rigidly, with his eyes on Professor Chown.

'What are you doing mixed up with him?' she asked, jerking her thumb towards the professor. The Rider stiffened, and his eyes darted sideways to look at Frankie, but he didn't answer.

Frankie thumped his arm. 'I asked how come you're riding around with the professor and his mates.' Through gritted teeth the Rider said 'it isn't through choice.' He clamped his lips shut, and re-directed his glare at the back of the professor's head. They were bowling along the M40 now, the motorway that cut a deep gorge between the Chiltern Hills, into Oxford and beyond. Catching Frankie's eye in the rear view mirror, Professor Chown said:

'Our friend has been my guest for some time now. We've had some very interesting conversations.'

Frankie dropped her gaze from the mirror, to stare at the Rider, who continued to glare at the back of the professor's head. *Is this what they call a "Mexican standoff"?* she thought, knowing the professor still watched her reflection, while she gazed at the Rider. The tension filled silence inside the vehicle increased as the miles sped by. Frankie swallowed hard a couple of times; there were so many questions she wanted to ask the Rider, but not here – not now.

Finally, Frankie heard the rhythmical click click click of an indicator blinking, and guessed they were about to exit the motorway.

The Rider swayed from side to side as the people carrier negotiated the twists and turns of a country road. Frankie wondered why he didn't take his hands from behind his back to steady himself.

Her heart rose into her mouth: 'He's been keeping you a prisoner?' She asked, and held her breath, wondering if Tony had noticed the Rider was handcuffed – then again, once Chown had made his surprise visit, Tony probably wouldn't have noticed a herd of pigs flying overhead.

Professor Chown swivelled to smile benignly at Frankie.

'I merely want to see a griffin before I die. Our friend,' he nodded towards the Rider, 'is being rather coy about introducing me to his griffin.'

Frankie's fingernails dug into her palms, glancing down, she saw her hands were curled into fists. She looked up again at Chown, fighting the urge to smack the silly smug smile from his face. She'd been right to suspect his motives from the very start – this was never about Michael – her mouth turned dry suddenly. Turning to the Rider, she whispered 'you told him – you wouldn't tell him where your precious griffin is – but you told him where I lived!' Her voice rose to a shout.

'No, I didn't tell him.' The Rider spoke calmly, and jerked his head to indicate Miss Gerraty. 'That woman there is in his employ. Once Chown has my griffin in his power, he won't need me anymore, and I'm dead.'

Frankie spun back to the professor 'Is this true?'

'Our friend has a vivid imagination.' Chown said smoothly.

'Do you deny you held Lord Leifur prisoner? Do you deny you stole the Wessex-Stone? Do you deny – '

'Shut up! Shut your lying mouth!' Miss Gerraty shouted, twisting in her seat to glare at the Rider. 'Lord Leifur *gave* Professor Chown that stone!'

' – A vivid imagination.' The professor continued, as though there'd been no interruptions. 'He's stubborn too. He wouldn't tell us anything. But at least I know the griffin's name. Who would have thought? Ballykinny Lad eh?' He chuckled, and dangled a red leather dog's collar in front of Frankie. Pointing to the Rider he said 'what's his name by the way?'

An echo floated through Frankie's mind. "*My name is Balkind's Rider,*" he'd said, and laughed. That warm September afternoon, which seemed so long ago now. The youth sitting beside her seemed a shadow of his former self. His hair was no longer white, but a dull dark blond. His skin was much paler too, as were his eyes. Frankie surmised he hadn't seen much sunlight in the past few months. His face was gaunter, making his cheekbones even more pronounced. As she surveyed him, his lips curled, with a sideways mocking glance she remembered too well, he said 'Stop staring little girl, I'm still the same man.' His eyes drilled into Professor Chown, but he addressed Frankie. 'I'm still Balkind's rider.'

With a jolt Frankie realised, that for whatever reason, the Rider *wanted* her to call Balkind for him. The Rider's eyes didn't leave the back of Chown's head, while Miss Gerraty glared at the Rider through the rear view mirror. Frankie concentrated on trying to remember where she'd heard the word Wessex before. It sounded so familiar, was it something to do with the youngest of the Queen's children? Something to do with Prince Andrew? She gasped suddenly: 'Lord Leifur – and the Wessex ley-line!' *Of course!* Luckily she'd muttered under her breath, only the Rider's keen ears heard her. He spared Frankie another sideways glance, and the slightest of nods. In her mind though, Frankie heard his voice again as he explained about ley-lines on that long ago September night.

"*Besides – Lord Leifur, the guardian of the Wessex ley-line, vanished to this world, over fifteen years ago.*" Frankie's hands flew to her mouth. No wonder Lord Leifur and his crystal had vanished – it seemed Chown had held him prisoner, just as he now held the Rider prisoner – but if Balkind responded to her cry ... Realising she was gnawing on a fingernail, Frankie whipped her hands out of her mouth, and thrust them into the folds of her skirt. With her hands out of sight, she crossed her fingers tightly, and prayed that Balkind would answer her call.

Gears grinded as Shaf shifted into second gear. They were driving up a steep road that climbed higher and higher. The indicator clicked again, and they pulled into a muddy car park overhung by trees, not much more than a glorified lay-by.

'This should do.' The professor said, ducking his head to glance through the windscreen. They were around a third of the way up one of the hills, about a mile or so away from the hill topped with the Victorian folly that marked the Devil's Hell Fire Club caves. The three adults began unbuckling their seat belts. Frankie glanced at the Rider as she unbuckled her seat belt, and mouthed 'Call Balkind?' The Rider, still with his eyes on the adults in the front seats, nodded his head slightly. His door swung open, and Shaf leaned in to unbuckle the Rider's seat belt, and hauled him from the people carrier. Frankie opened her door, and swivelled to make her exit from the people carrier; the ball gown slivered over the leather seats, and she sploshed down with both feet into a puddle.

Earlier that morning, when Frankie had walked Bally around the park, the grass under her trainers had been crisp with frost, and she had marvelled at the sunrise, brilliant swathes of bright yellows and reds bordering a cold blue. At this time of year, the sun barely rose high enough to clear the rooftops, hovering low in the sky and turning clouds a metallic bronze colour. The frost had almost melted, just a few sharp ridges remained across the muddiest ground, and Frankie's trainers squelched as she followed Miss Gerraty across the car park to access a pebbly path. Shaf and the Rider waited at the path for them, and Professor Chown followed, carrying a red and black tartan car rug. Frankie felt surprised when he draped it around her shoulders.

'Don't want our princess Francesca to catch cold, do we?' he asked, as though he were some kindly little old man, with only Frankie's best interests at heart. After a moment's indecision, Frankie clutched the rug tighter around her shoulders, and nodded her thanks. The goose pimples along her arms relaxed in the blanket's warmth.

'Straight up professor?' Shaf asked, encircling the Rider's arm with his hand.

'Straight up! Onwards and upwards my children!' The professor sang, as though they were all friends, out for a hike in the country. This hill wasn't quite so steep as other surrounding hills, nor quite so high. Even so, to reach the summit, even with the aid of the occasional steps cut into the hillside would be a trek for a seasoned hiker. Frankie needed one hand to hold her long skirt up, the other to keep the car rug around her shoulders. The backs of her calves began to ache under the strain of walking without being able to swing her arms for balance. Up ahead of her, the Rider fared even worse; he probably would have fallen were it not for Shaf holding him up. Behind her, she could hear strenuous breathing coming from the professor, and Frankie's own breath emerged as little puffs of vapour smoke. Only Miss Gerraty, alias Dr Perry, appeared unaffected, as she strode alongside Frankie. Her head bobbed, and her eyes darted from side to side, as though she were taking in the rolling scenery for the first time. Perhaps she was, but according to the Rider, she was in Chown's employ. If that were true, then from what Frankie could recall, the professor lived in Oxfordshire, and surely she must have at least seen the splendour of the Chiltern Hills from a car, or train. They were halfway to the summit now, and approaching a platform of level ground, before the slope became even steeper as it stretched to the summit.

'Here! This will do!' the professor panted.

Shaf stepped from the path, and pushing aside golden bracken ushered the Rider across the scraggy yellowing grass. Miss Gerraty and Frankie followed, the grass was sodden and Frankie's feet squelched inside her trainers. When she looked down, she saw the hem of the beautiful silk gown was muddied and bobbled with twigs and a few wrinkled leaves. She glanced over to the Rider, who stood feet from the edge of the platform, staring out into the horizon. His face was white and strained, but his eyes shone as he surveyed the glorious hills and valleys stretching away into the distance. As though feeling her gaze on him, he turned his head and grinned at her. 'Here would be a good place to call for your griffin.' He said.

Professor Chown shoved Frankie to one side. 'Take care of the girl,' he told Miss Gerraty as he scurried over to Shaf and the Rider. 'You – on your feet!' he snapped at Shaf, who was squatting beside the Rider. 'Get him away from the edge and make sure he doesn't try any "funny business".'

Shaking Miss Gerraty's arm off, Frankie walked to the platform's edge, halting a few feet away from the edge, and a few feet away from Shaf and the Rider. Frankie gazed out onto a magnificent vista; green brown and russet contours of hills stretched before her. Most of the slopes were rounded and smooth; a few had craggy rock formations dripping from their sides. She imagined the hills being formed, and some melting before they were quite set. She felt purged of all earthly cares, and took deep gulps of the fresh winter air. Her lungs burned, and her eyes stung, but she didn't care – she felt giddy with the wild beauty that surrounded her.

'Call him then, call the griffin.' The professor jabbed at Frankie's side with a bony finger. Frankie glanced at the Rider. A muscle twitched at the side of his mouth, but otherwise, he didn't move.

'Un-cuff him first.' Frankie said. Shaf reached into his trouser pocket, withdrew a bunch of keys and began to shuffle through them.

'Give me those!' The professor snatched the keys from the Sikh's hand, and thrust them into the patch pocket of his blouse jacket. 'Get on with it – the sooner the griffin responds, the sooner your brother can be on his way.'

Frankie tugged the car rug tighter around her shoulders. 'What happens if I call and the griffin doesn't come?'

'You'd better hope it does.' Miss Gerraty snapped. The professor held out a hand. 'Now now, Dr Perry, we have an agreement, don't we Francesca?' He peered into Frankie's face, and smiled. 'Call him.' Frankie stole another glance at the Rider. He could have been carved from stone, apart from his eyes, which flickered towards her, then back to the horizon.

"Call him Francesca, call with all your heart." Had he spoken those words, or had she heard them inside her head? No matter now, she stepped forwards, allowing the rug to flutter from her shoulders, and called Balkind's name out loud: Once, twice, three times.

Chapter nineteen.

'I've called, the griffin will answer. Now please – will you keep your promise?' The hills still seemed to echo with Frankie's voice, and somehow she knew Balkind had heard her summons.

'You mean, phone the fantastic Dr Dawson and have your brother transferred to Badaan Clinic?' Miss Gerraty sneered, looking down her nose at Frankie.

'That's what you promised – my mum – Tony – they're both with Michael now – they've signed all the paperwork! Professor Chown – if you don't make that phone call ...' her voice trailed off and an ice cold talon unfurled in her stomach. 'The paperwork's been signed – my mum's released our dad from all responsibility – Michael won't be able to stay on in the nursing home – there's nowhere else for him to go!'

Professor Chown raised an eyebrow, smirked at Miss Gerraty, and then smirked at Frankie. 'Come come my dear, let's not be so dramatic. I'm sure the National Health Service will find a bed for him, somewhere.'

Now the talon reached up from Frankie's stomach, to grip at her heart and her blood turned to ice.

She launched herself at the professor, knocking him to the ground. Straddling her legs across his prone body, she hammered her fist into his face – blood spurted from his nose – but not enough and she smashed her left fist against his temple and shouted 'You bastard, you bastard!' Shaf hauled her from Chown, still kicking and spitting, and clenching her fists. 'Let me go – I'm going to kill him!' She shouted, but the Sikh's grip on her tightened, crushing her arms against her body with one arm. Miss Gerraty knelt over Professor Chown, her hands fluttering around his head as though she dare not touch him. 'You guttersnipe!' she spat.

With one last massive effort, Frankie managed a feeble kick, and the tip of her trainer glanced off Miss Gerraty's chin.

'Lemme down – I'll kill 'em both!' Frankie tried to kick backwards, but now Shaf's other arm pressed against her windpipe, and she couldn't breathe. Frankie prised her fingers between his arm and her throat, watching as Miss Gerraty bundled her own coat beneath Chown's head, crooning to him, and dabbing her sleeve at his bloody and bruised face.

'Your griffin has answered your cry.' The Rider spoke.

What?! Frankie bucked against Shaf, and managed to swivel her head around to the Rider. His eyes were fixed on the horizon, he couldn't indicate with his hands, so he jerked his chin: 'Look – Balkind's answered your cry.'

Though Frankie never doubted the griffin would respond, her heart skipped at the sight of what could have been an overlarge kite, heading in her direction. 'Balkind,' she whispered, and blinked away sudden tears.

The pressure around Frankie's shoulders and chest lessened, then Shaf's arms dropped away, and he stepped back to shield his eyes as he too stared into the winter sky.

'Professor, Professor – please wake up – he's here – the girl's done it!' Miss Gerraty's voice pleaded.

Frankie glanced down at Chown's bloodied and bruised face. *Oh lord, did I do that?* She gulped down a mouthful of bile, and glanced away again quickly. A sheen, the merest glimpse of something metallic against the grass, nestling close to the Professor's waistband caught her eye, and her heart skipped a beat. Steeling herself against pity, Frankie looked back at Miss Gerraty. Her face, also blood smeared, tilted towards the sky, her hands supported Chown's head. His eyes blinked, then focused on a distant spot, growing wide in wonder. Feigning exhaustion, Frankie dropped to her knees, and pressed her palms against the scrubby grass. Under her left hand, she felt the cold jolt of metal. The keys! Scrunching her hand into a fist, she pushed herself upright. Only the Rider watched her – his eyes widened when she mouthed "quiet", and he looked away quickly, turning his gaze back to the skies.

Don't mess this up Frankie, don't mess up now! Her heart thumped, as her fingers stroked the keys – *yes – the handcuff key* – tiny against the other shapes. She stumbled forwards, careful not to interrupt anyone's view of the skies. A faint bellow sounded, but Frankie kept her head low, and circled around to the Rider's back. *Keep looking at the skies, keep looking up – don't look at me – don't look at me –* her heart pounding would surely give her away. With the tartan rug draped around her shoulders and dangling over her arms, she eased sideways to stand behind the Rider. His stance tautened, she touched his wrist, trying to give reassurance without words. Turning her body slightly to shield her actions, Frankie slid the key into the lock, and twisted; she felt rather than heard a click. A second bellow came, louder than before. She racketed the cuff's bracelets open, looking over the Rider's shoulder as she did so. *Balkind!* The ungainly dark mass hanging in the sky became rapidly larger. She watched for a second, tempted to shout out his name, loving the way his wings barely moved as he soared towards them. The Rider's hand grabbed hers, and spinning around, he sprinted away from his captors, dragging Frankie behind him.

'Hey!' A voice shouted – probably Shaf, but Frankie didn't look back. Clutching the handcuffs in one hand, and gathering her skirts in the other, she lifted them above her knees, and tried to match the Rider's pace.

Thank god I kept my trainers on! Studded football boots would have been better, her feet created mud slides, as they slipped and skidded against the grass. Somehow Frankie threw herself up the steep slope; when she stumbled, the Rider grabbed her hand, and continued to yomp upwards as though his life depended on it, yanking her along with him.

They'd almost reached the top of the hill now, two lovers smooching under a bush started apart in surprise as they raced past them. A high pitched scream drifted across the hill's slopes – Miss Gerraty giving vent to her fury. She staggered to her feet, and began giving chase, behind Shaf.

But Frankie and the Rider were racing along the summit now. Frankie's lungs were on fire, but the firmer ground meant she could sprint without fear of falling. Miss Gerraty changed her angle to intercept them. Frankie dragged her hand free of the Rider's hand, and yanking the tiara from her hair, she sent it flying through the air. Miss Gerraty ducked and dodged, glee on her face as she sprung upright again – in time to catch the heavy metal handcuffs which landed with a thwack on her long thin nose.

Whirling, Frankie snatched up her skirts, and chased after the Rider, her breath coming in short angry jabs which tortured her lungs. Puffing and panting, Frankie reached the Rider's side.

They were on the far side of the hill's summit; the Rider shielded his eyes with one hand, and smiled.

'Francesca – look – over there!' He slung an arm around Frankie's shoulder, and gently tilted her chin with his free hand: 'Look – your griffin has seen you.'

Two hang gliders circled below them, *they're about to get the shock of their lives,* Frankie thought, as she gasped for breath. But then her eyes fixed on the shape growing larger and larger, becoming recognisable as the one and only Balkind. The feeling of excitement and joy in Frankie's stomach was one she remembered from being seven years old and waiting for Christmas morning.

'He's here! He's here!' She screeched, jumping up and down and then she threw her arms around the Rider and hugged him.

A slapping of wings could be heard now, and Frankie breathed in the humid whoosh of air that preceded Balkind's approach. But Shaf had also arrived at the summit, and he held a dagger in his hand.

Balkind was a good ten wing flaps away; less than an arm's width away, Shaf raised his dagger to strike. In those few seconds, Frankie heard her brother's voice explaining that a Sikh's sword was called a Kirpan, and should only be drawn to defend the oppressed, and never used in violence. *You got that wrong, Michael.* She thought, flinching away from the long silvery blade.

The Rider pulled Frankie behind him, shielding her body with his. He didn't speak, but some form of communication passed between the two men. Seconds ticked by, Frankie held her breath; unable to take her eyes from Shaf's hand, the one gripping his sword: Would he attack the Rider first, or somehow barge the Rider aside, slit Frankie's throat and then step over her body to decapitate the Rider? Or would they both be frogmarched back down the slope and forced to grovel at Professor Chown's feet? Her eyes began to water; her ears began to ache, as she strained for someone, anyone to speak. No-one did. Instead, Shaf gave the smallest of nods, and his hand fell to his side.

And suddenly, Balkind was there, snuffling at Frankie's hair as he glided past, inhaling her scent.

Frankie giggled, and prodded the Rider forward, as Balkind's forelegs reached for the ground and made touch down. He crouched with his wings angled downwards, as if he sensed they had to make a quick getaway. They ran over to the griffin; the Rider threw her onto Balkind's back, and clambered on in front.

'Hold tight to me Francesca, try not to shift your body weight unless I do.'

Frankie's ears throbbed as Balkind's wings flapped, beneath her, his body undulated as the griffin paced forward, and she knew they'd run out of ground soon. She held her breath and closed her eyes, scrunching against the Rider's back. Something soft and warm enfolded her thighs. When she opened her eyes again, they were soaring above the ground. The innermost flap of Balkind's wings curled back along the griffin's flanks, and over her thighs. Provided she kept her seat, and didn't try wing walking or anything silly, it would be almost impossible to fall from Balkind. Surprisingly, because the warm humid air which always seemed to surround the griffin also engulfed Frankie, she didn't feel too cold. She had expected a chill wind to slap at her face, and her fingers to turn numb, especially considering the costume she was wearing.

'Francesca, hang on!' The Rider shouted, bending over Balkind's neck. Frankie tightened her grip around his waist, and bit back a scream as Balkind went into a dive. The Rider straightened again, and Balkind levelled out. When Frankie peered over the Rider's shoulder she saw Professor Chown, all injuries forgotten, running for his life, head up, arms pumping, and his bottom tucked in – trying to escape Balkind's wicked horns. She yelped with glee when Balkind's horns connected with Professor Chown's rump and he went tumbling down the hill's slope. Frankie yelped again as Balkind veered off, and climbed higher into the sky.

Without turning, the Rider tapped her knee. 'You can open your eyes now Francesca.'

Still clinging on to his waist, Frankie peeled her eyes open. Then let out a gasp of delight. They were soaring far above the Chiltern Hills and the Oxfordshire countryside all russet and brown spread beneath them. The freedom of moving in three dimensions was intoxicating. A thousand times better than any roller-coaster ride – no clanking grinding machinery and no spine jolting jerks. A dizzying exhilaration ran through her veins; Frankie thought she would burst with happiness. Then she frowned, certain they should be flying in the other direction. With Professor Chown's keys, the Rider could easily gain entry into his mansion and regain possession of the Wessex-Stone. They were flying over the outskirts of London now, perhaps the Rider intended to take her home before retrieving the lost stone of Lord Leifur. But then the neatly laid out grids of streets and roads of outer London were replaced by a greenness – and Frankie recognised the Round Pond of Kensington Gardens, seconds later they flew over the Serpentine River and suddenly they were flying over the pink strip of The Mall, and Buckingham Palace sprawled below them.

'We're going the wrong way!' Frankie shouted into the Rider's ear, as the glorious gothic architecture of the Houses of Parliament and Big Ben loomed to their left, and Tower Bridge hurtled towards them. The Rider shook his head, 'No, so long as I follow the River Thames, we won't be lost.'

The London Eye flashed below, skeletal white against the drab brown River Thames. With every flap of Balkind's wings, the width of the river increased. They flew over the Pool of London, and for the first time, Frankie saw the grandeur of London's Docklands – futuristic buildings made almost entirely of glass towered upwards, their images reflected faithfully by the Thames.

Minutes later the sky-scape changed – instead of seeing iconic shapes and domes beneath her, now Frankie looked down on the meaner street grids of the East End. They must be very near Romney Marshes now, all of London's bridges were behind them – the river had grown far too wide to be crossed by any ordinary span of bridge.

'You *are* going the wrong way – we're on the wrong side of London!' They would need to hurry to reach Professor Chown's mansion before him.

'This is the right way – Balkind's taking us to Michael.'

How could he know? Then Frankie remember the map she'd given the Rider, so long ago now it seemed.

'But you'll miss your chance – you can get Leifur's stone – you can return to your own world!' Frankie shouted against the Rider's ear.

'Calling your brother back into this world is more important, I think.'

'What?!'

'It is more important for you to call your brother from his world, right now anyway.'

'I didn't mean "what did you say?" I meant what do you mean?' *Oh lord,* thought Frankie, *what does he mean? What do I mean?*

But though he couldn't see her face, it seemed the Rider read her mind. 'I mean for you to call your brother from his world, into yours.'

'Wha... Don't be silly! Call him into this world?' Frankie laughed, but inside her blood simmered at the Rider's flippancy.

He twisted to face her, causing Balkind to dip alarmingly. 'Believe in yourself Francesca. If you can summons a griffin and his rider from another dimension, you can call your brother back into this world.'

'Turn around, turn around!' Frankie gibbered. With a smile and a shake of his head, he swivelled to face front, and Balkind's flight levelled. He didn't speak again, leaving Frankie to wonder over his conviction that she could somehow retrieve her brother from the limbo he resided in.

She prodded his thigh. 'I just have to call Michael's name?' *and whistle for him like a dog?* The Rider started to turn, 'face the front, face the front!' Frankie gibbered – her stomach had barely coped with Balkind's last pitch.

'I don't think it will be that simple, physical and mental contact is needed. And belief.'

Frankie shook her head, certain she'd misheard him. 'Mental contact?' She repeated, and then screeched as he twisted to face her again, and Balkind went into another crazy dive before levelling out. The Rider surveyed her, as though he wanted to search her soul.

'You can do this Francesca; Michael is lost in the world of dreamers. You must travel there, for him to hear your voice.'

'Enter Michael's dreams? How?'

'Make a physical connection, then make a mental connection, and then call your brother home.' As he finished speaking, he turned his back on Frankie without being prompted.

Oh of course, a mental connection: Silly me! Frankie told herself sarcastically. But another voice, not unlike the Rider's responded calmly: If you can summons a griffin, you can call your brother back into this world.

Chapter twenty.

Tony always seemed unshakable; but the look on his face as Balkind began his descent made up for all those times Frankie had failed to shock him. His eyes bulged, and his mouth gaped. He froze for a moment; and then a firecracker seemed to explode inside him. He hurled himself into the air with a triumphant 'Yes!' and sprinted forwards, skidding to a stop twenty yards from Balkind. He watched with awe as they dismounted, first the Rider, then Frankie. Then with another firecracker jump, he hurried over, his face alight with joy.

'You did it – you got your griffin back!'

Frankie was engulfed in an embrace, then just as suddenly released, as Tony walloped the Rider's back. His head swivelled towards the car park, and back to them: 'Where's Professor Chown – is he on his way?'

'Dad, I'm sorry – he was bluffing – there isn't any "miracle cure" – he lied to us.'

It was the first time Frankie had called him dad, but Tony's mind was obviously struggling with Chown's deception.

'But you called the griffin.'

The Rider placed a hand on Tony's arm. 'Professor Chown lied, but there's still hope. Your daughter can summon griffins from other worlds; Francesca can call her brother from his.'

Tony frowned. He opened his mouth to speak, but just then Balkind snuffled at his hair, and he put up a hand automatically to push away the griffin's snout. The Rider smiled.

'If you'd remain here with Balkind, I'd be most grateful.'

The courteous request surprised Tony into nodding agreement. Frankie and the Rider walked across the lawn and onto the patio; and as their trainers slapped over the slabs, Frankie saw her mum look up from Michael's bedroom window. She smiled at them, and then, as Tony had done earlier, her gaze shifted, undoubtedly searching for Professor Chown.

Frankie opened one of the patio doors and stepped inside Michael's room.

'I'm sorry mum, the professor lied.'

She gasped, and her hands flew to her mouth. After rubbing at her eyes furiously, she smiled again, a smile of resignation this time.

Behind Frankie, the Rider was unlatching the other patio door. He threw them both wide open, letting the sharp winter air chase away the antiseptic tang that was ever-present in sick rooms. Then he turned to Frankie's mum.

'Francesca is going to call your son back into this world,' he said.

Mum rose from her chair. 'What – '

Then she stopped. Now that she was on her feet, she could see what was taking place on the lawns outside. Wheelchairs zoomed across the grass. Even from here, they could see Tony had taken charge – organising nurses and patients into a queue, so they could pet Balkind one by one. Mum turned her head to stare at the Rider, now arranging chairs at Michael's bedside. He nodded for Frankie to sit down. Mum's head swung back again to the rumpus going on outside. The look on her face was priceless. Frankie bit her lip to keep from laughing out loud.

'Go and say "hello" mum – you might never get to meet a griffin again.'

Her eyes were wide and wondering, like a child's. Like a child, she nodded and without another word drifted outside as though she were sleepwalking.

Frankie watched her go. She'd spoken lightly to her mum, but her stomach twisted at the thought of what they were about to attempt. The Rider held Michael's dressing gown towards her, a question in his deep blue eyes. Frankie nodded, and shrugged her arms through the scarlet robe. Then she sat on the chair nearest to Michael's pillow, and took his hand, careful not to disturb the ever-present saline drip that prevented dehydration. Because Michael lay on a high hospital bed, with pillows propping him almost upright, their heads were level. Sometimes his eyes were wide open, staring without seeing at the window, or wall – which ever side he'd been turned to face. Thankfully, because that unblinking gaze unnerved Frankie, they were closed today. Every six weeks, nurses shaved his hair, for "hygienic" reasons. Michael would be pleased, if he knew – he always wanted a crew-cut but mum wouldn't allow him. She said it wouldn't suit him, and might make him look like a thug. Michael didn't look thuggish at all; his short hair looked like soft brown velvet.

The plastic chair beside Frankie creaked as the Rider also sat down. Without taking her eyes from Michael, Frankie asked 'How –' She licked her lips and tried again 'How do we do this?'

'Close your eyes and feel Michael's presence. Let images of Michael come to you. No matter if they're your images of him at first – he will sense that someone somewhere is calling him. By making physical contact, you will make it easier for him.'

Frankie blinked up at the Rider. *Could it really be that simple?*

His fingers brushed her face.

'Yes it really can be that simple,' – and Frankie didn't have to be a mind reader to know what he was thinking — "your thoughts show too clearly."

Taking a deep breath, and a last look at Michael, Frankie closed her eyes. Immediately a kaleidoscope of images jumbled through her mind, along with a horrific cacophony of shouting, screaming and moaning as a soundtrack.

Her eyes flew open, and she snatched her hand back as though scalded.

'I can't do this!'

The Rider's navy blue eyes surveyed her without pity and he spoke as though giving Frankie another grammar lesson:

'You can do this. What you meant to say is "I don't want to do this."'

A frisson of annoyance skittered through Frankie; and then she told herself to "man-up". If the Rider believed she could do this, then she could believe it too. Beneath Michael's closed eyelids, his eyes moved, as dreamers' eyes often will. Somewhere deep within that perfectly formed yet inert body, Michael waited for her to call him home.

Frankie placed her left hand over Michael's again, this time holding out her right hand for the Rider to grasp. He gave the briefest squeeze, and then simply allowed his hand to rest on hers, cool and comforting, while he stretched over to grasp Michael's other hand. Then he raised an eyebrow at Frankie to say "Ready?"

Frankie closed her eyes, and descended into Michael's nightmare again. Once more, images and sounds assaulted her mind. Imagining herself as a physical presence in this chaos, one wearing her usual jeans and trainers, Frankie put her head down and pushed through. Taking no notice of the mayhem that surrounded her, she concentrated on placing one foot in front of the other. Surely Michael would have created some kind of sanctuary for himself? If so, Frankie would find him there. As though someone had jabbed a finger at a remote control's off switch, the craziness stopped. Outside of Michael's mind, outside of this room, it was winter. Here it was mid autumn. Frankie walked through a field – sprays of bright red rose-hips sprawled over the hedgerow, and swollen blackberries hung from drooping brambles. The ground grew muddier and rutted with cloven hoof-prints as she headed towards a wide gap in the hedge, beyond which another field stretched away to the boundary hedge. A young girl appeared. Her golden hair hung to her waist, she wore a pale blue full skirted frock with a white pinafore over, and black shiny shoes, and Frankie knew her name: Alice.

Her hand must have twitched, she felt the Rider's hand respond with a slight pressure, barely sensed. *"Don't be scared."* Frankie didn't know if he saw her smile, but she did. Why should she be scared? She was in Wonderland with Alice, and she knew, somehow, that Michael had left this image especially for her. Still smiling, Frankie squelched through the mud, past Alice.

'He waited for you.' she said,

Frankie spun around, nearly losing her balance – She hadn't thought Alice's image would be able to speak.

'What?'

'He waited over two years for you.' The child's face and voice were solemn, just like the fictional Alice. *What am I thinking – the fictional Alice? This isn't real – none of this is real!*

A background groaning started up, and visions flickered: the madness wanted re-entry. Frankie concentrated very hard on Alice's clear blue eyes – willing herself to believe again – for Michael – that this was reality.

Alice gave a small smile of what Frankie thought was approval.

'Where is he? Where is my brother?' She asked, hearing a pleading note in her voice.

Raising her hand, still chubby with infanthood, Alice pointed upwards – towards the blackness of a woodland which filled the horizon. Frankie recognized the place immediately.

'Mad Mary's Woods?'

Alice nodded, and whispered, 'Be careful – *she's* got him now.'

Frankie turned to look at the woods again. When she looked back, Alice had disappeared. A scattering of leaves swirled, a handful of those became mired in the mud. Jewel-like colours from the autumnal rainbow's spectrum: Pink to darkest reds, pale golden to deep brown.

'Mad Mary's Woods are only trees.' She said out loud, and forged through the mud, to march across the next field. She clambered over the stile, and jumped down onto a cobble-stoned path. In Frankie's world, grass covered this path, with only the occasional glimpse of the stony ground beneath. The soles of her trainers slithered over the sharp stones; which were probably capable of ripping through thick denim and slicing into flesh. Hemmed in by hedgerows, with Mad Mary's Woods looming above her, Frankie tucked her head down and concentrated on keeping her footing. She caught the occasional flash of colour through the hedgerows, and two or three times shouts echoed. She didn't want to think of Michael, waiting in vain day after day, hoping for a glimpse of his sister. Neither did Frankie want to think about who "she" could be. But apart from a really annoying advertising jingle, she couldn't think of a single tune to whistle to keep her spirits up and her mind occupied. Instead Frankie mentally ran through her musical scales, starting with major and running through to pentatonic as she trudged along this seemingly never ending path.

A rustling and snapping of undergrowth startled her out of her daze. She'd stumbled into the woods without realising.

Frankie panicked – which way now? *If you lose your way in here, you'll never find your way home.* Once again, invisible fingers pressed against hers. *Stop that Frankie!* She scolded herself. *You know these woods – walk around the outside path, and then spiral inwards.*

Frankie *did* know these woods – but that didn't stop her getting lost in them every time she ventured too far inside. A song floated into her mind, an old music-hall ditty that she snatched at gratefully. Frankie began making her way through the woods whistling 'It's a long way to Tipperary' somehow feeling more confidence as she pushed on under a tunnel of trees where no autumnal colours glowed, only dark diseased branches.

Frankie reached the clearing where in her world there was only a pond or a marshy bog, depending on the season. In Michael's world, a much larger area had been cleared, and instead of just a fallen tree, a summer cabin stood to one side of the pond. Stone steps led down to a sunken garden, where a broad gravel path ran between privet bushes. At the far end of the path, another flight of stone steps led to a courtyard, approximately a third of the size of the garden. The manor house must be enormous, though from here it looked more like the world's creepiest doll's house. *Of course it wasn't crouching, waiting for Frankie to enter.* A white splodge appeared at one of the mullion windows, and then vanished. Seconds later a man appeared at Frankie's side. Under a flat cap his face was grey and lined with age. The broom he wielded ended in a collection of twigs rather than a bristle head, his knuckles were over large, and looked inflamed.

'Miss, don't go in there – go back – you're too late.' He muttered, pretending to sweep as he spoke. A bevy of creepy crawlies scuttled away from his broom; earwigs as large as earthworms, and Frankie's scalp prickled.

'What do you mean – too late? I'm Francesca Shaunessy. I'm looking for my brother, Michael Shaunessy. Have you seen him?'

The old man ignored her, his sweeping became more vigorous. Frankie placed a hand on his arm, surprised to encounter the unmistakable texture of wool. Beneath the old man's cardigan sleeve, was a pressure that spoke of flesh and blood.

'Go back now, else it'll be too late for you an' all.' The old man warned, shrugging Frankie's hand off, and sweeping the broom back and forth as though possessed. Her skin prickled with goose bumps – the idea that she could be trapped here in Michael's mind hadn't occurred to her. Then she gasped: This was no gentle pressure– small bones complained as someone clutched Frankie's hand fiercely. She'd startled the old man too. For the first time he ceased sweeping, and looked at her directly.

'If you won't heed my warning, then know this: she murdered her own babies, smothered them while they slept. She got her boy child back; now she wants her girl child back.' He smiled grimly, then glancing down, deliberately twisted the toe of his boot over a squirming earwig.

'Mary Howland is the most evil woman in this world or any other.'

Chapter twenty-one.

The elderly gardener glanced nervously down the stone steps, towards the gravel path; Frankie followed his gaze, trying to recall why the name Mary Howland sounded so familiar. The privet bushes lining the path sprouted from a single upright trunk, before bulging into uniform ovals of green. As Frankie stared at the bushes closest to her, features formed, and her heart sunk. She realised each privet bush had been carved into a clown's face. *No way! I can't do this – I can't* – to walk along that gravel path, between those silent sentries ... a breeze ruffled the bushes nearest to Frankie, and the clowns leered and smirked.

Quickly raising her gaze, Frankie looked beyond them, to the manor house. Once more she caught a glimpse of a white splodge at one of the windows. Someone inside the house waited for her – Michael? – Or Mary Howland? Frankie's blood froze as she remembered where she'd seen that name before. On a gravestone – the same gravestone that had plunged her brother into this purgatory. Frankie's stomach churned with fear, and she wanted to turn and run. Instead she took a couple of deep breaths, willing an anger to build up inside her, then channelled it into determination. Beside Frankie, the old man leaned on his broom, seemingly hypnotised by the clown/bush closest to them. Frankie shook his arm. He looked down at her, blinking, as if to say "You still here?".

'Is there another way to get inside the house?' she asked. He stared at her for so long Frankie thought he wasn't going to answer. Finally he came to a decision. With an abrupt nod, he said 'Follow me,' and started towards the summer cabin. Frankie couldn't resist looking over her shoulder, the clown's faces were just sculptured bushes again, dozing in the late afternoon sun.

Deep tracks rutted the ground between the pond and the summer house. Frankie could just make out a faint impression of horseshoe prints between the tracks. The gardener finished unlocking the summerhouse, and waited patiently.

'They drag ice from the pond in the winter months, and we store it down here – in the ice room.' He explained, responding to Frankie's unasked question.

'Oh. I see.' She didn't really, but entering the summerhouse, Frankie saw two oversized handles bolted into the floor at the far end. Grasping the handles the gardener strained, and then lifted up a section of floor and placed it against the wall. He beckoned Frankie over with a jerk of his head. She peered into the hole, a few feet of polished wood was visible, before it vanished into blackness.

'We chuck the ice down here – into a cellar. There's a tunnel from the butler's pantry in the big house – saves having to bring the ice out into the sunshine during the summer – see?'

They crouched on opposite sides of the hole, peering down the chute. Chilled air chapped at Frankie's face and she shuddered. It must be incredibly cold down there.

'There's barely any ice left, you should be alright.'

Frankie wanted to snivel. Instead she sat down at the hole's edge, with her heels against the chute. Easing her backside onto the start of the chute, she pushed off with her hands before she could think again. Her feet hit the ground with an ankle jarring thud, and she yelped. A blackness engulfed her. Frankie groped behind, feeling for the smooth wooden chute at her back: and surely this time the Rider read her mind; Frankie not only felt his hand squeeze hers, but heard his voice. 'Courage Francesca, have faith.' So instead of trying to scrabble back up the chute, she stood up with her arms outstretched and her heart hammering and stumbled forward until her finger tips brushed against a wall.

'A tunnel, the old man said this was a tunnel. Walk forwards, and you'll be fine.' She whispered to herself. Gingerly, she inched her way along the tunnel, sweeping her hand along the wall, not daring to lose contact in case she became hopelessly disorientated. The blackness was complete – no glimmer of light to hint at which way was up or down, let alone backwards or forwards. Every step she took jolted up through her ankles and into her knees. She tried shuffling her feet, but the scrabbling of her own trainers against the compact dirt floor of the tunnel chilled her blood, and could be muffling the sound of someone, or something, shadowing her. She walked as silently as she could, along this long cold dark seemingly endless tunnel. Her scalp prickled, and the back of her neck felt horribly exposed to anyone, or anything that might be creeping up behind her. Now and then her hand encountered the soft sticky residue of an unknown insect, or spider's web; Frankie kept her tongue curled against her teeth in an effort not to shriek. At last the toe of her trainer buffeted against wood. Frankie edged her hand from the wall, breathing a sigh of relief as her fingers traced the trim of a door frame. She reached out with her other hand, and stroked the wooden panels, until the shock of cold metal against her palm indicated she'd found a door handle. Holding her breath, she grasped the handle, and levered it downwards. She pushed against the door. It wouldn't budge. *Silly! Doors swing open outwards from rooms!* Taking two steps back into the darkness, she lowered the handle again, and pulled.

A russet glow blossomed into the tunnel, Frankie's heart hammered faster – she'd made it! She'd reached the kitchen. She eased herself around the door, pulling it closed behind her. For a few seconds, she paused, and glanced around the room. Filling her vision was a large rectangular kitchen table. Several oak trees must have gone into its construction. Behind the table, a wrought iron fire basket as large as a baby's cot sat inside a fireplace, that seemed roughly about Frankie's own height. Frankie stared into the glowing embers, and saw the outline of charred logs, before her eyes stung and she had to look away.

Great – nice going Michael! She thought – *first "Alice in Wonderland", now "The Victorian Kitchen!"*

She moved cautiously into the room, freezing when a door slammed and a maid scurried into the kitchen from the garden. Her hands were red and swollen, and clutched a bunch of carrots. Throwing them onto the kitchen table, the maid picked up a kitchen knife. With deft motions, she topped and tailed the carrots, and began scrapping the dirt from them.

Frankie stepped forwards, the maid shrieked, and the knife clattered onto the table.

'Oh miss, you scared me!' She pressed her hands against her chest, and giggled nervously. Frankie smiled back 'I'm sorry – I didn't mean to startle you. I'm looking for – '

' – your brother.' The young maid finished for her, picking up the knife to resume her chore. Frankie watched the blade flashing over the carrots, then glanced up at the maid's face.

'Where is he? Where's Michael?' Frankie asked, stepping closer to the table. A lank tendril of brown hair curled from the maid's old fashioned mob cap. She pushed it back under the cap, and her eyes darted to and fro: first right, towards a door, and then back to Frankie. Leaning over the table as far as she could, the maid whispered 'He's upstairs, in the classroom. Go up one flight, and turn left, it's the second door along.' Then she bent her head over the carrots, and the knife flashed again.

Feeling bemused, Frankie headed through the door, into a hallway panelled with polished dark wood. Stern men and women glared out from gilt framed paintings lining the wall. Three broad stairs led up to a half landing, and the first flight of stairs continued at right angles, along the wall. Frankie ran up the stairs, not bothering to be stealthy, it seemed she was expected. She hurried along the corridor, and without knocking, flung open the second door she came to.

Sunlight flooded through arched windows, throwing patchwork shadows against the opposite wall. Girls dressed in old fashioned frilly dresses with matching ribbons in their hair, and boys wearing calf length trousers and page-boy style haircuts sat on wooden benches: There were four children to a bench, and in front of them, another long stretch of wood at chest height served as a desk.

'You're late. Come in and sit down quietly, Francesca.'

Frankie clung onto the door handle, feeling light headed. When her dizziness subsided, she turned her head towards the voice's owner. A woman dressed in an elaborate snowy white blouse, tucked into a long dark skirt, poised in front of a blackboard which was supported on a wooden easel.

'Are you ...' Frankie swallowed hard, licked her lips and tried again. 'Are you Mary Howland?'

'Miss Howland, or ma'am if you please! It's rude to stare, close your mouth and take a seat. Don't make me cane you.' The woman's voice and face was clear and gentle. But her eyes drilled into Frankie's, and when she smiled, Frankie caught a glimpse of jagged yellow teeth.

'I'm not here for a lesson, I'm here for my brother.' Frankie dragged her glance away from the woman, and tried to decide which of the pasty thin faces was her brother, Michael. Had the maid misdirected her? The eldest child here only looked about twelve. One of the boy's hands shot up into the air. As he strained towards his teacher, almost begging for her attention, his floppy brown fringe swung forwards. He thrust it from his eyes with an impatient flick of his hand, and Frankie yelled out his name 'Michael!'

Mary Howland moved like lightening, grasping Frankie's hand by the fingertips, she swished a long willowy stick downwards. Before Frankie could react, a searing pain shot through her palm, Frankie blinked away tears, then yelped as the woman nipped Frankie's ear between her thumb and finger, and dragged her along the room. She shoved Frankie into a corner.

'Stay there – or else!' Another thwack sang out, Frankie wanted to turn her head, but felt compelled to face the wall. Then a chanting started up, led by Mary Howland's clear voice. 'Once one is one; twice one is two ...' Frankie began giggling hysterically – multiplication tables – her idea of hell!

Turn around now, you have to turn around and break the spell – else you'll end up like one of them. She told herself. *Michael's my brother, and I'm taking him home – she has no right!* Summoning up all her will-power, Frankie slowly pivoted on the ball of her left foot. The children's mouths opened and shut in unison, their glazed eyes were fixed on their teacher. All except one. In the second row, Michael clasped his left hand against his side, and stared at his sister. His eyes implored her not to do or say anything that might get them into more trouble. 'Michael,' Frankie whispered. He shook his head, and raised a finger to his mouth. 'Michael,' Frankie raised her voice, and stepped away from the wall '– you have to come with me, you don't belong here.'

The class continued chanting, their voices droned on: "Three twos are six, four twos are eight ..."

'Michael – please – ' Frankie continued walking towards her brother as if in a dream. The class continued to chant – drowning out her pleas. Frankie clambered over the first desk, pushing aside two girls with their hair tied in identical pigtails. The girls' eyes were fixed and staring, and they continued to chant. Miss Howland's skeletal fingers dug into Frankie's shoulders, and the spectre roared with rage, smothering Frankie's senses with fetid breath.

Frankie concentrated solely on her brother: 'Please, please, Michael – you have to listen to me, you have to come with me.' Frankie implored him, trying to make eye contact. But Michael stared through her, as though he hadn't heard. The pressure on Frankie's shoulders increased, she flinched against the steely grip, and almost cried out. Frankie shook her head, trying to clear it of the hypnotic chanting of the children, and the red starbursts of pain.

'Michael, please Michael – I can't go home without you.' She sobbed out loud, steel rods drilled into her shoulders, and her heart beat in time to the childish voices counting: 'four fives are twenty, five fives are twenty-five ...'

Frankie bit down on her own lip savagely, the sudden shock diverted her mind from the chanting, and the painful vices at her shoulders.

'Michael – look at me!' She screeched 'It's me – Frankie – and I've come to take you home!' She screamed as Mary Howland managed to hook her leg around Frankie's legs, trying to knock her off balance.

'Michael – please – I need you – we need you!' She flung herself forwards again, stretching out to her brother. Then amazingly, Michael's hands stretched out towards her; Frankie grabbed them, and clung on so tightly, her knuckles turned white. 'Don't let go Michael, don't let go!' Frankie shouted to make herself heard above the insane chanting.

Michael's face turned whiter, his own fingers tightened around Frankie's, as Mary Howland yanked her backwards once more.

'Cheska, don't let me go,' he shrieked. Tears spurted from Frankie's eyes at this old pet name. Twisting her head, she opened her mouth and bit down savagely into Mary Howland's wrist, hating the squelch of rotten flesh between her teeth. Immediately the vice at her shoulders disappeared, but seconds later Frankie's scalp was on fire as Mary Howland tried to lift Frankie by her hair. Frankie kicked out, and Mary Howland let out a "whoof" behind her. Straining every muscle in her back, Frankie flung herself backwards, dragging Michael across two desks with her. Michael had always been taller than her, sometimes only by a fraction of an inch. But as Frankie helped her brother find his feet, she saw she was now the taller twin. She glanced at Mary Howland, and smiled. The woman clutched at her stomach, doubled over with pain. The other children never faltered in their chanting, their eyes never left Mary Howland's face.

Still holding Michael's hand, Frankie ran from the classroom, and along the corridor. They clattered in tandem down the stairs and into the kitchen. The tunnel door stood open, the kitchen maid beckoned them forward with a whirling motion of her arm: 'Quickly – I'll lock it after you've gone!'

Frankie rushed into the tunnel without hesitation, Michael's hand felt warm and sweaty in hers. With two of them, they could reach either side of the tunnel walls, and it seemed seconds before they were out of the tunnel and into the ice house. Letting go of Michael's hand, Frankie took a running jump at the wooden chute. Gnarly hands grabbed her wrists, swinging her up into the summer house. Then Frankie and the gardener crouched down to haul Michael up. The elderly man's face creased with joy. 'You got him then!'

Frankie pushed back her hair with both hands, and grinned at Michael, then the gardener. 'You should know, it's never too late!' The old man shook his head 'You're not out of the woods yet – come on.'

Michael was staring around him with wide eyes. Grabbing his hand again, Frankie followed the gardener out of the summer cabin, suddenly anxious to be clear of Mad Mary's Woods. As they hurried past the sunken garden, the old man cupped a hand around his ear – and now Frankie heard it too – the thundering of hoof beats. Michael clutched at her hand and pointed 'Look – she's coming for us.' A black horse galloped towards them, nostrils flaring and its mane flying as it churned up the distance between them. Mary Howland's hair had escaped from its bun to stream behind her, and her skirt flapped wildly around the horse's foam covered flanks.

'Go! Run! I'll hold her up.' Before Frankie could protest, the old man hoisted his broom like a lance, and charged down the steps. Michael dragged at Frankie 'Come on – don't let his sacrifice be for nothing.' They were running hand in hand again, behind her, Frankie heard a frantic neighing, and a woman's scream.

'Don't look back Cheska!' Michael panted, as they pounded along muddy paths, ducking and flinching from overhanging branches. Up ahead was the stile leading to the field where Alice had waited. 'Not far now.' Michael panted again. *Why did he need me?* Frankie wondered, and then she remembered how scared she had been in the tunnel, and knew Michael would never have broken free of Mary Howland's spell, not without Frankie to deliver a good kick to the woman's stomach. They were over the stile and racing towards the muddy gap between the hedges now. Frankie bounded forward, and once again almost toppled over, as a sudden weight dragged at her side. Still clinging onto Michael's hand she twisted to see what held him back. He was knee deep in mud. Slapping her other hand over his, she tugged with both hands, but Michael was stuck fast. A triumphant howl sounded, and Frankie looked across the field to see Mary Howland descending on them. Her hands hooked into claws, and her lips drew back, revealing those terrible yellow teeth. Sensing Michael was trapped, she howled again, and seemed to double her pace.

'Cheska – let go – run – leave me here!' Michael shouted. Sobbing, Frankie refastened her hands, this time around Michael's wrist. She pulled and strained with all her might, using every last ounce of strength – 'No Michael, no – I won't! I wont let you go!'

But Michael was trapped firmly, the soft gluey mud might as well have been solid concrete around his feet and legs. Frankie lifted up her head and screamed silently into Mary Howland's face, only yards away now. The spectre faltered, and its features twisted with bewilderment.

'I won't let go – I won't let you go!' Frankie tightened her grip around Michael's wrist, then gasped. With a breathtaking pain, the bones in her right hand grinded together and she screamed out loud. In the quietness that followed a voice said 'You can let go now Francesca,' in a calm authoritive manner. Still she clung onto Michael, feeling tears prickle at her eyes, and then scald her cheeks.

'Hello Cheska.' A second voice said. It sounded gloopy and came out: 'lo Eska,' but it jolted Frankie's heart. She opened her eyes to see her brother smiling dopily at her. His gaze shifted to the Rider, then over to the open patio doors and his smile broadened. Seconds later, Frankie's mum hurtled past her, and snatched Michael into an embrace that went on for ever. Finally she let go, her face shiny with tears and she leaned over to hug first Frankie, then the Rider. Frankie couldn't bear to take her eyes from Michael; he looked shyly at the Rider, then at Frankie and then shrugged as if to say "Mothers!" But when mum hugged him again, he hugged back.

'I'll go and get Tony.' Frankie said, getting up from her chair. Immediately the ground beneath her shifted, and the room rotated. She clutched at the Rider for support. 'Steady there,' he smiled 'You've been visiting other worlds. Sit down again, I'll bring your father over.' Frankie sank back into her chair gratefully. Mum perched on Michael's bed, with an arm around his shoulder, stroking his hair and murmuring to him. Michael's bewilderment and dizziness must be far far greater than Frankie's, but he seemed to be coping better than her. He couldn't take that soppy grin off his face, and his large brown eyes sparkled with glee. Frankie's cheeks ached with smiling. Feeling drunk with happiness, she made an effort to sober up a little by looking away. Her eyes wandered around the room: There were two doors at either end of the wall opposite, one leading into the main corridor, one to an en-suite shower room.

Clustered between the doors was all the stuff Michael wouldn't be needing anymore. A row of monitors, a medical trolley with sanitary equipment on the top shelf, and needles and drugs in the locked cupboard underneath. Above the monitors and trolley Tony had hung a shelf, mainly for the cards and photographs from Michael's friends. There were birthday cards too; Michael and Frankie had turned sixteen on the 12th of December. *We can have a proper celebration now*, Frankie thought. Both the shelf and the room were painted white, so objects appeared to hover mid air. The stone which had formed the centre of Michael's mineral collection seemed especially gravity defying. With a black glassy surface, it generally just sat there like – well – like a lump of rock. But now it glowed. Frankie stared at it, transfixed, she watched veins of red appearing and disappearing, as though writhing to be set free from the blackness. Flashes of red wire flared, broadened and stretched and then dwindled away again, but she couldn't focus on just one strand – the whole rock was alive with them. Puzzled, Frankie tottered over for a closer look. She stretched out her hand towards the rock, then hesitated; a faint warmth and a vibration pulsed in time to the red threads. Just then, the door banged open. Startled, Frankie grabbed at the shelf for balance, and then groaned with dismay as one of the supports gave way, and everything slid in slow motion to the floor. But before she could stoop to pick up the cards and photographs, Professor Chown stormed into the room, a startling white plaster over the bridge of his nose. The two police officers shadowing him stood awkwardly in the doorframe. Frankie glimpsed mum's startled face, then shrieked as bony fingers dug into her shoulders. She kicked out at Chown's shins, but he hung on with surprising strength. Mum shouted 'let go of her' and started up from Michael's bed. Michael cowered back into his pillows, and Frankie felt a twinge of pity for his confusion. The tallest policeman stepped forward, holding up his hand palm outward, trying to calm the situation. But then Tony and the Rider entered through the patio doors. Professor Chown's hair stood up from his scalp, 'arrest that man!' he screeched. His fingers dug into Frankie's shoulders, and he jiggled on the spot with fury. 'Arrest him!' He screamed again.

'Sir, please calm down.' The plump copper still propping up the doorframe warned.

Meanwhile in a seamless movement, Tony pushed the Rider behind him, pressed Frankie's mum back onto the bed, and stepped around to the tall policeman's side. 'Take your hands off my daughter.' He snarled. Chown gave Tony a dismissive glance. 'She's coming with me! Officer – arrest that young man!'

The Rider now stood beside Frankie's mum. She clutched at his hand, while still embracing Michael, but she appeared poised to fly across the bed and tear at Chown's eyes. She never got the chance. Tony's fist smashed into Chown's nose. Frankie heard a grunt, then the pressure at her shoulders eased, and a weight slumped against her back. Tony grabbed her before Chown's body knocked her over, and pushing Frankie to one side, Tony pulled his warrant card from his back pocket.

The two coppers appeared relived someone senior was taking charge. 'Take him back to your station, I'll be along later to press charges. For now, attempting to abduct a minor and endangering vulnerable adults should suffice.' Frankie grinned when Tony added 'You've certainly got plenty of witnesses.'

After a few minutes of confusion, the two policemen left, dragging Chown between them. He'd regained consciousness, and a trolley wasn't needed. Tony was the new star of the show. Mum looked at him with gleaming eyes and Michael managed 'Way to go dad.' Like a toddler, his speech dropped the first letter of nearly every word, but the meaning was clear. Tony sniffed loudly, and muttering something about going to find a doctor, ducked out the room.

The Rider disentangled his hand from Frankie's mum's grasp. Nodding towards Frankie, he touched Michael's hand gently and said 'I'm pleased you made it back to your own world. Now I must go and rescue Balkind from his new friends, and leave in search of my world.'

A flitter of unease crossed Michael's face. Frankie hurriedly said 'Balkind the griffin, not Balkin the dog.'

'Griffin?' Michael mouthed, his speech deserting him completely.

Frankie smiled. 'It's a long story,' she wanted to add 'and you're going to love it' but at the moment there was no happy ending for the Rider. Frankie's eyes met his, and he smiled – a cheeky smile. He dangled Professor Chown's keys from his fingers.

'I've time enough to retrieve the Wessex-Stone, thanks to Tony.' He bowed towards the door, which as if on cue, opened to admit Tony. 'Doc's on her way.' He muttered, his eyes were no longer watery, but red veins showed on his face. Which reminded Frankie – 'Leifur's stone – does it look anything like this?' Ducking under Michael's bed, she gasped in surprise, then hurriedly stretched to retrieve the black rock. Only it now glowed with a redness that had an unmistakable heat.

Scrabbling backwards and to her feet, Frankie held it out for the Rider's inspection. His eyes widened. 'The Ella-Stone!' She'd surprised him for the first time ever.

'Is that what you need to get home – back to your world?' mum asked anxiously.

The Rider nodded, he too had lost his voice.

Michael followed this avidly. He swallowed hard, and all four of them spoke at the same time. 'Take it.'

Frankie giggled, they sounded like a Greek chorus. Placing the rock in the Rider's hands she repeated 'Take it, if you need it, it's yours.'

He gazed down at the rock with an expression of wonder, it appeared to glow with a life of its own. Then he looked up at Frankie: 'You don't know what you're giving away. This is priceless – it can enable a traveller to go between worlds.' Frankie glanced over at Michael. Mum was encouraging him to sip from a plastic beaker, while Tony retreated to the en-suite shower-room, sniffing softly.

'I think we've made a pretty fair swap.' She folded his fingers around the rock, and standing on tip-toe, brushed her lips against his cheek. The Rider nodded again, a dazed expression on his face.

'It really is that simple.' Frankie teased him. His eyes sought hers, and she glimpsed a flicker of fear.

'Come with me.' He blurted, and her mum who had no business listening in, shouted 'No!' The Rider started, then recovered himself and with a small bow in mum's direction said 'Not back to Ella-Earth, but I would desire Francesca to travel with me to yonder ley-line.' He nodded towards the patio windows, as if they could see the nearest ley-line from here. Perhaps the Rider *could*, with the Ella-stone in his hands.

'Mum, please – ' Frankie tried begging.

For the first time, the Rider seemed lost. Without being told Frankie knew he worried that even the Ella-Stone wouldn't be enough to help him get home.

'Now then Lu-Lu, let's not be too hasty. We owe this young man.' Tony stepped back into the room, blowing his nose noisily. Shoving the tissue into his pocket, he surveyed the Rider. 'How long will it take you to fly out to this Ley-line?'

'I would return to Leybridge. Francesca will be waiting for you at home.' Tony nodded. 'Okay – I'll follow in the car, you'll probably have to wait for me, Frankie.' Mum started to protest, and Michael stared at his sister with undisguised envy. 'Fly on a griffin? You lucky cow!' He twisted around to look at Tony 'Can I go too?'

'No you can't!' Their mum answered for Tony. Addressing the Rider she said 'You take care of my Frankie, mind you fly slowly.' Biting her lip to keep from giggling, Frankie pushed the Rider through the doors and out onto the patio, before anyone could change their minds.

'Thank you, I promise Balkind will fly slowly. Goodbye, and good health and luck to you ...' The Rider continued to make his farewells as Frankie hurried him out onto the patio and then across the lawns towards Balkind.

They skirted wheelchairs, and pushed their way through a mass of starched nurses' uniforms, and doctors' coats to find Balkind playing to the crowd. His eyes were closed in ecstasy, and clear juices dribbled from his mouth, as his lower jaw moved from side to side, accompanied by loud slurping noises.

'I told you he'd like pears!' A small boy in an overlarge pushchair shouted. Opening his eyes, Balkind ignored the Rider and Frankie completely, and craned his head towards the next offering.

'No madam, thank you, but chocolate cake isn't very good for griffins.' The Rider placed his hand over Balkind's snout, lowering the griffin's head, and with the other hand, pressed against Balkind's shoulder. Balkind automatically sank to his knees, and in one fluid movement, the Rider swung onto his back. He beckoned for Frankie to mount behind him. But first, she plucked a silvery feather from Balkind's wings, which were already expanding, and passed it to a girl in a nearby wheelchair. She was Frankie's age, and her hands were clasped and entwined together, but she managed to grasp the feather between her fingers, and looked at it with shining eyes. When she whispered 'thank you' her companion gasped, and Frankie wondered if Balkind had worked another mini-miracle. Before she could respond though, the Rider called her name. Balkind's wings were fully inflated now, and he was shaking them out to their full size, ready to begin his take off. Frankie scrambled onto his back, behind the Rider, laughing as Balkind snaked out his head and snatched at the forbidden chocolate cake.

Chapter twenty-two.

As though rehearsed, the crowd surrounding Balkind retreated four or five paces. Mouths opened and closed, most of the on-lookers were jumping up and down, Frankie guessed they were cheering. She could only hear the slap of Balkind's wings against the air, as he prepared for flight. Frankie's adrenaline raced, coursing through her veins and she could barely wait to be soaring through the air again. The air grew heavier, and warmer; a lot warmer. The two spinal like columns that ran from Balkind's snout, over his broad head and along his neck extended along his shoulders and back. Behind the Rider, Frankie nestled comfortably in the slight hollow between these two ridges. Their legs dangled down Balkind's flanks like Native American riders. Frankie echoed the Rider's movements, leaning into him, as Balkind soared into the skies. Even without any form of saddle, they sat securely, even more so when Balkind's body levelled out. His wings, those folds of skin inflated by blood vessels and trimmed with feathers, hooked backwards against his flanks, flowing around their legs.

The freedom of moving in three dimensions once again rushed to her head, Frankie decided it was a million times better than any roller-coaster. One long ago holiday in Cornwall, a freak tide had ripped into their part of the Atlantic ocean, creating monster roller-coasters of an unusual warmth. Frankie and Michael had plunged into the frothy waves, allowing their bodies to be buffeted and swirled, leaping and diving through the waves like dolphins. Frankie was reminded of that magical time now, only she didn't have to keep her mouth closed, or hold her breath; they tumbled and glided through air as Balkind rolled with the thermals.

The sensation of pure joy continued, as they flew towards the setting sun, skirting London and flying over the home counties, now the Rider knew his way back to Leybridge. They'd left the nursing home far behind, and Frankie wondered if the Rider still felt this dizzying sense of freedom. She leaned forward and shouted 'This is awesome!' The Rider whooped and laughed, and seconds later Balkind zoomed into a dive; Frankie could no longer catch her breath as hilltops rushed towards her at a horrifying speed. Finally managing to gulp air into her lungs she let it out again in one long 'eeeeeeeekkkkk!' Balkind was flying level again and she could no longer see directly beneath her as his wings obstructed her view. They swooped over hedges and fields, close enough to see the bovine faces of cows, as they stretched their necks to moo their disapproval. Balkind bellowed back, a friendly bellow of greeting. Frankie grabbed at the Rider's hoodie: 'Up, up!' She gibbered. He laughed again; Balkind's wings angled away from his body, leaving Frankie's legs feeling terribly unprotected and she clutched at the Rider for dear life. Moments later they were gliding majestically once more, and the earth below resembled a green blanket with blue and grey streaks marking rivers and roads. Frankie breathed a sigh of relief. Somehow, soaring above the ground at this height wasn't so scary as flying with the ground racing yards below them. But the Rider hadn't finished showing off yet. Frankie yelped and flung her arms round his waist as Balkind darted to one side, then another, dipping first one wing, then the other. Suddenly they were zig-zagging through the sky, with Balkind performing little bounds upwards, tossing his head up and down like a dressage horse.

'Stop it now!' Frankie shouted, not that she was scared or anything – just that Balkind might hit a rogue air pocket, or tire himself out, and in any case: 'You promised my mum...' Frankie reminded him. Still laughing, the Rider's shoulders flexed, as he gave Balkind another command, and they were flying smoothly again. Frankie wondered how the Rider communicated with Balkind, and decided either the Rider was a fantastic griffin rider, or Balkind was very well trained, or more likely they were in perfect harmony with each other.

The setting sun shone directly into Frankie's eyes now. Looking down; if she strained to see over Balkind's wing span, she could glimpse an outline of the ground below them. In the middle distance she saw a broad swath of hills, one of which was topped with a Victorian folly of a church. They were within sight of the Chiltern Hills and fast approaching Leybridge village. The hot fetid air that always surrounded Balkind's flight increased in density. Frankie's head began to ache, pounding in time with a primal throb that came from the ground, still hundreds of feet below them. The thrumming collided with the crystal the Rider carried, and magnified to an unbearable level. Waves of electricity rolled through the air, seemingly attracted to them, and Balkind's flanks heaved as he strained to remain airborne. His wings flapped against an unseen barrier and Frankie noticed the Rider's hair hung damply around his neck. When she reached up to touch her own hair, it sizzled and Frankie just knew it had curled into a mess of frizz. With agonising slowness, Leybridge drew closer. As they descended, the meadow became steeper, steeper than it had ever seemed before: it could have been man made rather than natural. The last of the sun's ray stroked against the sky, creating a burst of yellows and reds that smeared themselves into a glorious sunset. Even as Frankie savoured the spectacular colours, dark clouds began rolling in from right and left, marring the picture. On impulse, Frankie glanced behind her: bruised looking clouds followed the griffin and his passengers, blotting out the last of this pale winter day. It felt like the end of the world.

Despite the heat radiating from Balkind, Frankie began to tremble uncontrollably. The Rider touched her knee briefly. *'Don't be scared.'* He said without words. Balkind did his trick of hovering in the air, and his wings tacked against the air. His front legs stretched and seconds later he gambolled on firm ground, with his wings half folded. Immediately, Frankie missed the comforting blanket around her legs; the chill night air hit her skin as though someone had opened a nearby freezer door. Frankie shivered as Balkind came to a halt, bringing all four legs underneath him with a military precision. The Rider patted her knee again, a signal to dismount, but Frankie couldn't move. As soon as she dismounted, her griffin and his rider would fly off, and she might – *she would* – never see them again. She choked back a sob, trying to control herself, and clamber off Balkind's back. She hesitated too long. The Rider grunted, and manoeuvring his leg awkwardly over Balkind's neck, jumped down. He threw his arms up to catch Frankie, and placing her hands on his shoulders, she slithered off Balkind's back. Still clinging onto the Rider, she looked around Six Acre Meadow, so familiar, yet different somehow.

'So, this is goodbye.' Frankie pushed a swath of hair back from her eyes, and tried to smile.

The Rider looked down at the crystal, still glowing in his hands, and frowned. He glanced at the sky. There was no thunder, but flashes of electricity darted back and forth.

'I was foolish to bring you here,' he said, with a baleful look towards the base of the tor; towards the church. 'You shouldn't be here.'

Frankie hugged him. 'I wouldn't have missed this for the world.' But her voice came out strangled. The Rider gently prised her hands from his shoulders. 'Francesca, hurry back to the church. Wait for your father on safe ground.'

She frowned. 'What's happening? When you came through to our world, I didn't even realise Balkind was there until he started flapping his wings.' Tipping his head backwards, the Rider surveyed the skies again. The clouds billowed, threatening and full of malice. 'I don't know. Maybe because I'm forcing a way through, while you simply called.' He looked down at her again. 'Promise you'll get off the meadow, away from the ley-line?' Frankie nodded agreement, wrapping Michael's dressing gown tighter around herself. The Rider's eyes sparkled with mischief. 'And promise you'll never call my griffin again?'

Frankie sighed, and Balkind sensing discord, nuzzled her hair. 'I can't – I can't ...'

'Be brave Francesca, Balkind belongs in his own world, and so do I.'

He smiled, and stooped to kiss her forehead, then without warning, hurled himself onto Balkind's back. Bellowing, Balkind reared, and wings flapping he gambolled forward, and within a few strides took to the air again.

Chapter twenty-three.

If there was a cloud making factory, it had gone into overdrive, puffing out mis-shapen marshmallows which billowed across the sky; great banks of clouds from a bright silvery grey to a bruise colour of purple black. Frankie's hair streamed out horizontally, and she struggled to remain standing upright – but there was no wind. She disobeyed the Rider, in any case, she couldn't move. She kept her eyes on Balkind's shape as his wings flapped, carrying griffin and rider higher and higher.

Lights played across the clouds now, scarlet and vivid green. Directly overhead, but miles above, an puddle of blackness appeared. The clouds swirled around this hole in the sky in an inverted whirlpool, and the blackness spread, growing larger and larger as the clouds spiralled away. At the centre of the blackness, a tunnel of whiteness opened. Frankie's heart beat faster – surely this was the membrane separating! They'd done it! She whooped, and jumped, and then stood on tip-toe; Balkind and his rider were going home!

'Yah-haaaaa!' the scream rippled from Frankie, and she almost overbalanced. Recovering herself, she strained every sinew, and held her breath, willing the crystal to create a path home for the Rider and Balkind. But plainly she wasn't needed. The fuse was lit, and the sky blazed. Balkind's wings continued to swipe at the air, as he climbed towards the rift between worlds. Frankie waited for a flash of lightning, or at least a roll of thunder, but one moment a griffin shape could just be seen, the next – nothing.

'You did it. You did it.' She whispered, and she crumpled to the ground, crushed by desolation and aloneness. On her hands and knees, she threw her head back and yelled into the darkness for Balkind. 'Balkind! Come back – oh come back; Balkind, please come back.' She couldn't bear being in this world without him.

The ground still hummed with latent energy, lights still played across the clouds, surely it wasn't too late?

'BALKIND!' Frankie yelled, but the electric lights narrowed from thick ribbons to strands that were barely there. The clouds began to roll across the skies in an orderly fashion, the humming subsided, and she was alone.

Still on her hands and knees, Frankie dropped her head and wept, shuddering with each sob. Eventually, she could cry no more. 'You're a big girl now,' she muttered, and staggered upright. Wiping her face with the back of her hand, she scanned the skies again. A faint milky glow marked the place where Balkind had disappeared. 'Gone, all gone.' Frankie mourned, and started back down the meadow, slowly, because her legs didn't seem to belong to her.

Slipping and sliding, Frankie headed straight down the glassy slope, ignoring the path which curled around the meadow's side. If she fell, so much the better: she would reach level ground quicker. She wanted to go home, climb into bed and pull the duvet over her head, and stay there forever.

A blast of humid air engulfed her, a rouge hot spot, no doubt. But some little part of Frankie must still have hoped, for she turned – and Balkind's head and neck rushed past her, his wings barely a foot from the ground. Air buffeted around Frankie, knocking her to the ground, she twisted her head upwards to see Balkind circling for a second approach.

'Frankie!' Someone shrilled her name. It was her mum, rushing up the slope towards her, Tony must have broken every speed limit to drive home this fast.

'I'm sorry mum, you've got to let me go – I'll be back – I promise!' Frankie stood up. This time Balkind's approach was gentler, he glided alongside her. The Rider stretched out, and snatching up her skirts, Frankie grabbed his arm, and vaulted onto Balkind's back. She wrapped her arms around the Rider's skinny body, and looked back down the hill towards her mum. *Please mum, understand – I have to go with them!* Mum's arm rose, in a semi-salute, and Frankie's heart almost broke for her. But then Balkind wheeled, flying higher and higher towards the milky membrane, already melting away as the rift repaired itself.

The Rider spoke, sounding exasperated: 'Lady; I would care to know the enchantment you have placed on my griffin.'

Frankie hugged him tighter. Her heartbeat raced at a terrifying speed and she felt dizzy with exhilaration: she was flying into an unknown world, but she was with *her* griffin, and the Rider, and he'd called her "Lady".

The air grew frigid, ducking her head against the Rider's back, Frankie wrapped her arms even tighter around his waist, huddling up to his body heat. Beneath her, Balkind's flanks heaved as he struggled for breath, each down stroke of his wings took a lifetime and she'd ruined everything, behaving like a jerk. Then the world changed. Frankie couldn't see anything, but she didn't want to see anything. The stillness and absolute nothingness frightened her beyond anything – even the thought of giant spiders. She couldn't breathe, and didn't want to breathe, for fear of what she might inhale. They were travelling through a void. A voice sang out, nonsense words, and Frankie realised it was the Rider singing to his griffin. His braveness warmed her slightly, but they were still between worlds. If Balkind couldn't find his way through this tunnel that shouldn't exist – all three of them would cease to exist too. Or maybe they would be doomed to flit between worlds for eternity. Frankie's chest tightened at the thought. Still Balkind's Rider sang: For certain he made the words up but his voice rose and fell with Balkind's wings. Frankie convulsed, forced to take small shallow breaths, and she clung onto the Rider for dear life. The rough fabric of the Rider's rucksack chaffed against her cheek, and something dug into her– the crystal! It must be digging into the Rider's back too. Frankie sobbed. This wasn't fair! It was the hardest thing she'd ever had to do in her life, un-tucking her head, unfastening her arms, and sitting upright to loosen the rucksack's drawstring neck. Even during the deepest underwater dive in Trey Lake, Frankie was still aware of some sensation against her skin. Here there was nothing, and it was more than soul destroying: The void was feeding on Frankie's soul. From far away, like the very faintest of dreams from a long ago childhood, she heard the Rider's voice, still crooning. "Balkind is a good griffin, the best griffin, when he gets home he'll have his dinner, big dinner, nice dinner ..." Because the Rider promised his griffin, because the griffin believed, somehow Frankie dug a little deeper and found a last smidgeon of strength. She rummaged through the Rider's rucksack, until her hands felt the smooth warmth of Lord Leifur's stone. She withdrew the stone carefully, and then held the crystal out at arm's length. A crimson beam shone, pushing the relentless milkiness away, inviting the blessed darkness to replace the nothingness.

Balkind's flanks still heaved, but his wing strokes became firmer, more determined. Frankie could see the outline of his head and neck, a darker shadow against the black. They'd made it! They'd crossed from one universe to another. A searing flash of brilliant light forced her to close her eyes. When Frankie opened them again, she saw a canopy of blue above her, reflected by the ocean below. Probably Balkind meant a huge joyful bellow, but he could only manage a croak. The Rider's hand slapped against Balkind's neck 'Clever griffin! Good griffin!' he cried, his voice choking with emotion. They were heading towards a cliff formation now, a street of water gushed over burnt orange cliff-tops. As they neared land, the torrent of water drowned out all other sounds; a building being demolished couldn't have made more noise, only this crushing tumbling discordant symphony would never cease. The Rider's shoulder dipped, and Balkind's wing dipped, and he circled the cliff top, starting on his now familiar descent.

Balkind landed with a butterfly touch, but then his forelegs crumpled and the Rider shot over the griffin's withers, and hit the ground with a back-flop. Frankie braced her palms against Balkind's shoulders, where the thick veins of Balkind's wings emerged. Gritting her teeth against the shock that jolted through all the tendons in her arms, she peered down to see the Rider, spread-eagled on craggy ground, staring up at her with a look of surprise. Frankie choked back a giggle. The Rider's expression changed from shock to outrage, he glared up at Frankie; not a good move when you're flat on your back and your dignity's in the dust. The giggles became hysterical, between hiccups of laughter Frankie managed to say 'Stop it! Your face – it's priceless!' She knew she should dismount and help him up, but the sight of the proud confident Rider with the wind knocked out of him was too funny for words.

Just as Frankie managed to control her laughter, the Rider recovered enough to roll onto his hands and knees and stagger upright. Immediately he began dusting himself down, and then stooped to recover his rucksack. Biting her lips; Frankie slipped down from Balkind's back. The Rider grinned sheepishly, then throwing out his arms and tipping his head back he yelled 'we're home!' He pirouetted a full circle, and facing Frankie again, threw his arms around her, and hugged her, lifting her from her feet. 'We're home!' he shouted again, against Frankie's ear. She hugged him back, and somehow his lips brushed hers, just for the briefest instant, and then he buried his face between Frankie's neck and shoulder. 'We're home.' He repeated softly, against her skin. Frankie's bones turned to liquid, her legs trembled, and she wanted him to kiss her again. A snort of disgust fluttered against Frankie's hair, as Balkind's head snuggled on her shoulder. Stepping away, the Rider smiled down at Frankie, and patted Balkind's snout.

'I promised Balkind the meal of his life. We'd better make a start back to camp.' His smile faded, as he surveyed Frankie, and then his griffin. He rubbed at his own cheeks, then straightened his tee-shirt and dusted his hands along his track bottoms, as though aware he too was travel grimed and dishevelled. He raised his eyebrows, and then turned and started down the craggy mountainside. Frankie heard a muttered 'Ye gods, have I got some explaining to do.' Balkind followed, with his head down, and his wings clamped to his sides. Frankie's cheeks burned at the Rider's rudeness. She clutched at the crystal for comfort, and counted slowly to ten, breathing in the soft fresh air of this new world.

Then she hurried down the mountainside to catch up with the Rider and her griffin.

<<<<<*****The end*****>>>>>

All rights reserved. This book may not be reproduced in any form without written permission from the author.

Julia Hughes is the author of "The Celtic Cousins' Adventures":
"*A Raucous Time*", "*A Ripple in Time*", and "*An Explosive Time*".
In addition to these three Celtic Cousins' Adventures, Julia's other titles include the romantic novella: "*The Bridle Path*", and a seasonal short story "*Crombie's Christmas.*"

Website for: Julia Hughes
Website for: Talon Publishing

Author's acknowledgements:

With very grateful thanks to Dody, who I think in another life will be a griffin rider, that's my wish for her anyway.

Thank you Sean, and a special thank you to Dan; together the Campbell brothers make a formidable pair, and are extremely generous with help and advice.

Deepest thanks to Stephen Spencer, namer of griffins, and the best critique partner ever.

Sincere thanks to Jenny Worstall, for her invaluable advice on all the musical references, and a big thank you to Charlie Plunkett. These two lovely and talented ladies donated their time as proofreaders, and I'm extremely lucky to call them both my friends.
Grateful thanks to J B Johnston who's professional proof reading services are highly recommended:
www.brookcottagebooks.blogspot.com
www.facebook.com/brookcottagebooks

Lastly, thank you to my boys: I wouldn't miss the ride for the world.

You make it all worthwhile.

Julia Hughes 24 March 2013

Printed in Great Britain
by Amazon